FRIENDSHIP?
WHO NEEDS IT ANYWAY!

FRIENDSHIP?

WHO NEEDS IT ANYWAY!

Sue Norris Janetzke

XULON PRESS

Xulon Press
2301 Lucien Way #415
Maitland, FL 32751
407.339.4217

www.xulonpress.com

Printed in the United States of America

Paperback ISBN-13: 978-1-66281-342-9
Ebook ISBN-13: 978-1-66281-343-6

This book is dedicated to my husband,
my best friend and the love of my life.

I miss you, but I know God has a plan.

Table of Contents

Chapter One

The End

THIS IS THE WORST DAY OF MY LIFE. I CANNOT BELIEVE that I am only fifteen, and everything I have worked and slaved for is now gone and nonexistent. My life is over, or at least it might as well be over. This is the end of life as I know it. I never thought Dad was serious about taking a job away from here. I cannot believe he did. I know God has a plan, but right now, I do not understand it.

Parents - they never understand anything. How could they do this to me, make me move from my hometown to another one? So what if my dad got a new job? The new place probably doesn't even have a college or shopping mall or even a decent theater. I wish I was dead. I can't believe we are moving.

Parents can be so unreasonable. As hard as I try to convince them to stay here in Chicago, they are unmovable in their decision to leave. I thought I had it all worked out where I could stay here during the week. My best friend Betty said I could stay and live with her and visit them on weekends, but, oh no, I had to move with them.

I never thought my parents could be so selfish. I bet they never had to give up the world's greatest and most popular best friend just because somebody said they had to. And now I have to miss the ninth grade going-away dance, and all the fun Betty and I have will be over. What about my boyfriend Jonathan? I'll never find another boyfriend as cool, good-looking, and popular as him anywhere else.

I might as well be dead. It would be less painful. That stupid city, Grand Rapids, probably doesn't have a theater group. I didn't work so hard and long to be the lead in last year's production just to move away and go unrecognized again. Honestly, my parents have no consideration for me at all.

My sister Samantha, age 11, thinks it's great that we're moving. She finally will have her own room and won't have to share it with Sarah the baby (we call Sarah the baby, even though she is three. I guess that's because she still sucks her thumb and carries around a blanket). Sam gets something out of this move - a new room. All I'm getting is headache and heartache. Oh, so you think Jonathan will write to me? I wonder if I'll have to give him back all the stuff he's given me. Oh, brother, everything in my life is just a terrible horrible mess.

Sarah doesn't have an opinion yet. As long as we bring her blanket and favorite toy, at the moment, she could care less. I cannot believe that my parents never even considered asking me if I wanted to move. They just decided all on their own. I hope I will not be so self-centered when I'm a parent.

I suppose that we'll be moving into a real stupid neigh-borhood with ugly girls and uncool boys, or else just all little kids. At least I'll be able to babysit and get some money. After all, I will probably never be noticed or ever have another date again. With no life, I guess babysitting will help fill my empty lonely time.

Well, I said my said good-byes to my friends, and Jonathan. Oh, yeah, he'll text, call and keep in touch. I know that is a BOLD-FACED LIE, but it made me feel a little better.

I hate fifteen. I can hardly wait to be sixteen. That has got to be better than this. I am not looking forward to tomorrow.

I dreamed all night about Chicago, friends, ball games, shopping, and fun. How could any other place make me as happy as I have been in Chicago? Grand Rapids couldn't possibly be this perfect. What will it be like, this place, the Snowbelt of Michigan? Snowbelt? I can hardly wait to find out what that means.

Chapter Two

The Move

IT'S MOVING DAY. I CRIED ALL NIGHT AND ABSOLUTELY refused to talk to my parents, the "Rents." my new pet name for them. I won't change that name until they at least apologize for what they are doing to me. I vow from this time forward to speak only when spoken to or until they recognize what they have done to me and are sorry for doing it. I hear Mom calling me, reminding me not to forget anything and that the movers are here. I find it hard to believe that she wants to move either. Come to think of it, she did give my dad that "look," and he didn't yell at me after I sassed him back about not letting me stay at Betty's to live instead of moving. I wonder what Mom really thinks about this move? Oh, no, it's really happening. The movers are here.

It is now evening of this awful day, and I am thinking again about Mom. Mom's not so bad most of the time. You can't talk to her about sex or anything like that, but she's always there if you need her, and she shows up to everything we sign up to do. She never gets on my case about my weird friends either, so maybe this move is hard on her too.

I keep thinking about her asking me if I forgot anything. OF COURSE I HAVE. I left a room where I felt safe and comfortable, where I tried out my first pair of heels and started my period, and had conversations with my best friend about my deepest thoughts. I feel as though I left a piece of myself there when I walked out. I couldn't even shut the door. Shutting the door would make this move seem so final. When I walked out, I could feel tears spilling out of my heart. I had been a child there. Does that mean that now I am grown up?

Leaving the bedroom door open, I walked to the steps and down the stairs. There was my mom at the bottom of the stairs. She couldn't talk either. Grabbing me, she gave me a hug and we walked to the car together where everyone else was. Neither of us could say a word.

Everyone else seemed so full of anticipation: Dad grinning from ear to ear, Samantha talking a mile a minute, and Sarah all wrapped up in her blanket, sucking her thumb. Mom looked so solemn, and I did all I could not to cry as Dad pulled out of the driveway, down the street, and away from Chicago, Illinois, my comfortable place. We went on our way south and then east, toward Grand Rapids, the Snowbelt capital of Michigan. I wonder what that means.

Chicago had been such an exciting place to live, so alive with culture and events, ball games and friends. I was never bored there. How could any other place be as friendly and make me as happy as I had been here in Chicago?

The trip took six hours as we expected, and since the movers were expected a couple of hours after us, I decided to explore the house when we arrived. It couldn't hurt to look, and it didn't signal my approval or anything.

Mom went to the grocery store with Sarah and Samantha, and Dad sat on the floor of the living room, since the furniture hadn't arrived, to read a paper he had picked up at our last rest stop. I was content to wander around and discover what the house they had chosen had to offer. They had shown us pictures and described the house and the neighborhood, but I was too mad and upset to act interested. I certainly didn't want to let them know that I approved in any way of any decisions they had made without consulting me. Dad left me alone in my solitude as he read and kept his distance.

The house itself didn't look too bad; quite a change from our three-bedroom two-story to a four-bedroom ranch. The living room was considerably larger than our last house had been, and here we had a dining room too. Now we had four bedrooms, and I had been promised the first pick because I was the oldest. The three bedrooms on the main part of the house looked already taken. I knew the larger one with a bath off it should be for the Rents, as much as I would like to claim it. The other two near that one were sort of the same size as the rest. One had a large walk-in closet, and it caught my eye, but it reminded me so much of Samantha because it was pink. The smaller one had just the right shape to it for Sarah's trundle bed.

Walking down to the basement, I saw the bedroom located there and knew immediately that it was perfect for me. It had a large double closet, small window, and plenty of room for my double bed, desk, and bookshelf. It had to be mine; it was perfect for me. I loved it instantly because there was so much privacy. Already I could envision my pictures and posters hanging up, a large mirror, and Jonathan's picture on my dresser. If only I could convince my dad to put a lock on my door, then everything would be perfect.

I ran upstairs and asked my dad about the room, and he told me that they had agreed I had first choice, so if that was the one I wanted, that was the one I could have. Finally, things had begun to look up for me. Something had gone right. The basement also had a recreation room with a fireplace, and I was sure the Rents would let me have a party down there when I made some new friends. Things were looking a little brighter than they had looked two weeks ago. Maybe I would eventually get used to this place. To be on the safe side, I thought I should continue to keep my vow of not speaking to them just in case I continued to be miserable. I was going to have a hard time remembering to be quiet as my excitement over the possibilities for my room grew alive in my head.

As soon as Mom, Sam, and Sarah arrived home with burgers and fries from a local burger place, Grand Rapids did not seem quite so backward now, knowing they at least had a fast-food place. Mom had located a large shopping mall, theater, high school, middle school, and had driven by several churches. It helped knowing that we were not out in the desert with only a slight breeze, wild animals, and no water. I was beginning to feel a little bit safer, but not comfortable as of yet.

A few hours after the hamburgers and fries had been consumed, the moving van arrived, complete with all of our furniture and the rest of our prized possessions. By the next day, at least the furnishings seemed familiar and made me feel a lot more at home. Now I could finally text some interesting things to Betty and Jonathan. I tried to remember not to text anything I wouldn't want my sisters or the Rents to read.

Remembering Memorial Day weekend was coming up, I thought about past holidays in my comfortable place and wished I was there. It's pretty nice here, but I refuse to let the Rents know that I feel that way yet. I love my room with my furniture and stuff moved in; it feels warm and almost comfortable. I have not met any kids yet, although I feel as if someone is continuously watching me. It's a very strange feeling. Maybe I can figure that out tomorrow.

After a few days, I discovered not too far from our house there were places to go where I could shop and get away, just by walking. This was great. I could walk to the corner and use my phone and talk in privacy. This had definite potential. My Rents were pretty reasonable about letting me go off on my own as long as they knew where I was going to be. This helped me to walk off a lot of resentment, disgust, and anger that I still couldn't control. Sometimes I would get upset and not even realize that it was coming on or why I was upset. These walks helped me calm down inside as well as outside. I did enjoy exploring the area on my own and checking out the local stores. I know with my phone, the Rents could track me, so I didn't wander too far, and I had to keep track of my allowable phone minutes or they would take the phone way. This time was needed for me, and it helped me feel more independent instead of resentful. Maybe I could make this work. I have to remind myself that God has a plan.

Chapter Three

Adjusting

THINGS ARE ACTUALLY GETTING BETTER. SINCE I HAD ONLY two weeks left at the other school and Mom had convinced Dad to let me go back and stay with Betty for those last two weeks, life seemed better. I still missed the farewell-to-junior-high dance, but at least I had a few last moments with Jonathan. I guess what I began to feel was a type of closure. This helped me put an end to Chicago life and a beginning to Grand Rapids life. Mom pulled through once again for me. Sometimes she is amazing.

Jonathan had given me a special necklace with a broken heart on it, and promised he'd always love me. This made it easier to leave, knowing he was miserable too. He was just too cute, and I was really going to miss him.

Betty and I managed to squeeze a summer's worth of talk into those last two weeks. We discussed what will be happening when we turn sixteen this year. You know, sweet sixteen and never been (short line here); you get to fill in the blank with whatever you want. I've been kissed, but never have done a lot of other things so far, and I don't want to either. I am still curious about those other things, and so is Betty. We vowed to tell each other everything that happens to everyone, who does what and when, and if we are doing anything and when. I am really going to miss her. I will never find anyone that I can talk to as well as I can talk to her. She understands me, and best of all, she knows how to keep things to herself.

Since being allowed to go to Betty's, much of my resentment about the move is starting to fade. After all, we had promised to keep in constant contact, so nothing would be allowed to change without our agreeing to let it change. I actually started looking forward to meeting some new kids, longing to decorate my new room, as well as to continue to check out the new neighborhood. I hope God's plan is one I can follow, instead of making my own way. This is hard.

Chapter Four

Make New Friends

BEING BACK AT THE NEW HOME, I WAS ABLE TO MEET A FEW of the neighborhood kids. One of the girls a street behind us is a cheerleader, and since I used to be one, I hoped that maybe we would become friends. Her name is Shauna, and she looks like a cheerleader...long legs and arms, and long brown hair, much cuter than I am, for sure, and she seems nice. I don't really trust beautiful girls who are nice, but she introduced me to a couple of other kids, so I guess she's alright. At least I will know a couple of kids when we start back to school in the fall. She seems to know a lot of people. I wonder if that means I need to watch what I say to her. The funniest thing is that she lives kind of behind our house, and she watches people with her binoculars. Maybe I wasn't imagining things when we first moved in. She might have been watching me then. I'll have to ask her when I get up my nerve.

Shauna showed me around everywhere and seems to know everything about everybody and everything. I wrote Betty all about it, but I haven't received a letter back from her yet. I wonder if she misses me. I haven't heard more than just a few short texts from Jonathan either.

School starts in just four days. I don't know what I'll be interested in here yet, but Shauna's interest's centers around cheerleading and boys. She may be full of information about people, but I have had a hard time finding out about any other kinds of information from her. Some of the information my mom had sent to the house told us a little bit about the school's extracurricular activities, which is what I wanted to know more about. The school's pamphlet focused more on sports and academics. There was not much in it about clubs, music, or other after school activities. It just mentioned that they had other activities, not what the activities were.

I intend to go to college, but I would rather have fun before I do. The extracurricular activities are what make school work for me. Without them, I will not be able to function, survive, or live. I try to keep my grades at a B- level or above, and then the Rents do not yell too much, and I do not have to kill myself studying. Shauna feels even less committed to grades than I do. She plans to go to college too, but all she really wants to do there is meet men, date, and finally get married. A career is not on her list of goals to achieve. Her parents have a lot of money, and Shauna just does not worry about the future, money, or a job.

Shauna's boyfriend this week is Allen. He is last year's captain of the football team, a junior, and he is gorgeous too.

They make quite a cute couple, kind of like Barbie and Ken, with more action. Allen set me up with one of his football buddies, and we double dated with them. Rich is a senior who played wide receiver. He was cute too, but when I would not do "it" on the first date, Rich decided I wasn't worth his time. I could not very well tell him I had never done it, so I just pretended it was too soon to get that romantically involved. He was pretty self-centered anyway. All he talked about was football, what a terrific player he was, and how some college was just going to snatch him up after this fall's season. Some of these guys think they're God's gift to women, and what a kick in the head it would be if we ever told them what they really mean to us. He was not much fun anyway, so I did not mind at all that he never called me again.

I couldn't stop thinking about our double date. What was Shauna really like? Does she do it on the first date? Does she even do it at all? The way Allen was drooling all over her in the back seat left little to the imagination. No wonder Rich was in the mood! Maybe Shauna does everything but do it. I guess I will have to get to know her better before I know the answer or can speculate on an answer. I wonder what Rich told Allen after they dropped us off.

The next day, Shauna informed me that cheerleading tryouts were going to be the next week. I can't decide if I want to make the attempt to try out for the squad. She has encouraged me to try out and has tried to teach me some of the cheers at East Grand Rapids High School. None of the cheers she has taught me were familiar, and none were cheers that we did back at good old Mount Hope High in Chicago. These cheers seem to focus more on dance and the beat and some acrobatics. At Hope, it was different. I am glad that I took dance for three years in sixth, seventh, and eighth grades. Even though the classes were a long time ago, without them, I know I would have been practically lost. Fortunately, I catch on fast, and that will help me be ready by Monday's first practice session. I do want to make a good impression. Back at the old school, I was pretty popular, but here, I'm starting from scratch. Shauna says she will put in a good word for me. That should help as kids seem to flock around her when we go places. I guess I am pretty lucky to have found such a popular person to be my new best friend. It is really nice that I like her a lot too.

This place is working out all right so far. Sam has made friends with some of the girls from the church we have been attending. Pastor said that they have an active youth group and I should join, but I want to wait and see what Shauna does and what my other new friends do. This church seems to be all right. The minister is not too preachy, and the music is pretty good. A lot of the kids that I have met go there, and Shauna and her family are members there, but do not go much. Mom is getting involved in a lot of the activities with the women's group and the children's Sunday school people. I think that will be good for her to make some friends too. She has looked sort of depressed lately.

Dad has been gone a lot at work at his new advertising job for Klancies. One good perk is that he always gets free samples, and we all love their elves cookies.

Mom enrolled Sarah in a play group, and she will start preschool in the fall. Sarah is happy as a lark since we have a swing set at this house, and she can play outside all she wants. Since the backyard is fenced in and the gates are locked, she can go in and out of the house off the kitchen deck, play outside, and come in on her own. She seems to be enjoying this little piece of independence. There's a little boy named Robbie next door that is her age, and she seems always eager to be over there, or he is over here. This keeps her quiet, not to mention happy, and Robbie's mom goes to the same church, so she and Mom have become good friends. So far, everyone seems to be adjusting to this move with little resistance, even me.

Next weekend, we are going to have a picnic with the neighbors. Shauna gets to come with her folks, and Robbie's family and a couple of the other neighbors. One of them has twins the same age as Samantha, so she is really on cloud nine now. She knows five whole people that she will be attending school with.

Sarah and Robbie were a stitch at the picnic. They decided to wash the swing set without asking, and soaked the entire backyard, themselves, Samantha, and the twins. It was lucky that it was such a nice warm day.

Shauna and I got away for awhile and went over to her house and used the binoculars. We watched the party - you can see our house great from there, and we also boy-watched for awhile.

Allen snuck over, and I kept watch while he and Shauna were alone for a few minutes. He brought another friend of his to keep me company. Of course, this friend, Ted, was another football player. Ted, fortunately, had a steady girl-friend, so we got to talk a lot. He seemed like a nice enough guy. It was real comfortable just talking to him. They only stayed about fifteen minutes as we were expected to be back soon, and Shauna was afraid of getting caught. She should be - she looked slightly tussled when Allen left. It must have been an active fifteen minutes.

The party was just shutting down when Shauna and I returned - talk about close calls! Since school was to start the next day, the party wasn't expected to last long as everyone was returning to their own homes. Sam went to dream of her new classmates, Sarah, the swing set, and me - my thoughts were focused in so many directions. I figured my dreams would be a mismatch of acting, cheering, dating, and visions of the unknown. If I was lucky, one of my dreams would become real, and I would find it perhaps the next day at school. I know God has a plan, I really believe that, but I hate not knowing. I hate waiting. I need to pray for patience.

Chapter Five

School Begins

HERE IT IS, THE FIRST DAY OF TENTH GRADE. THE HALLS here resemble those at my other school – things always are so clean the first couple of days; pretty soon, there will be scuff marks everywhere and litter in the halls. I can hardly believe that I lived through the summer and that it is time for high school. I had looked forward to being in high school, and I hope that it lives up to my expectations. Not only am I looking forward to meeting some more kids, but I'm dying to find out how to get into the choir, and of course, following that, will be the school drama club or Thespian Club as it was called at my other school.

After receiving my horrible schedule - no drama, no choir, just garbage classes like geometry, English, US history, biology, French II, and stupid study hall, I feel totally depressed. My first-hour teacher, Mr. Nurfed, told me to go directly to the counseling office to see how I could add drama or music. I should be able to drop his study hall class and add choir easily, I hope. Mr. Nurfed said that if my transferred grades were acceptable, I probably would be able to drop the study hall.

My counselor, Ms. Strump, said there would be no problem adding choir, all I needed was to get the choir/music teacher to recommend me and she would make the change. She gave me a pass, and off I went to find Mr. T. Timpson to sing my heart out. After I answered his questions and did the vocal tryout, he signed the form to let me into the choir. Thank God, I can now live a full and productive life, or at least be in one class I can't live without.

Choir seems terrific, and there are over one hundred kids in it. I sing first alto as well as second soprano, and I sit next to a senior named Abby. The choir consists of all three grades, inter-mixed, and no one gets in without trying out. Noticing that about half the choir consisted of boys, I already had my eye on Bill, the tall tenor, with the deep set dark brown eyes. Unfortunately, I found out at lunch from Shauna that he's going steady with Elaine Willoughaby and has been since the seventh grade. I guess I will keep looking. I am dying to see who this Elaine Willoughaby is. Shauna says she's in choir too, so I should be able to figure it out pretty soon.

The French teacher, Mrs. Swaynie, spent all hour discussing French and its relevance to our world, while picking lint off the front of her skirt. At least she was entertaining. I imagine I will not get much over a C in here as it looks like a real boring class. Besides that, Mrs. Swaynie must be as close to one hundred years old as they allow teachers to get before they have to retire. Maybe I'll get lucky and she'll retire mid-year. At any rate, all she talked about was how much fun the spring Leaning Tower of Pizza party would be for those students who earned As or Bs all year. She went on and on about what a magnificent addition it would make to our calendar and what a memorable experience it would be. It almost makes me want to avoid those grades just so I'll have an excuse to miss this great event. Just the same, it does not hurt to have an open mind, and after all, I do want to go college, and Cs just do not help a person's grade point.

My next class was biology with dreamy Mr. Pender. He is single (I asked) and not gay (at least no one thinks he is). I just love hands-on classes like this. We get to dissect frogs, grow plants, and do many other things with animals, and studies about animals. It will be very interesting, I can tell. The best part is that he sits us in alphabetical order, and Serena Joxmer goes right beside Bill Johnson. Maybe I will make a new friend after all. Watch out Elaine, there's competition in the ranks, and your precious Bill may just be in for a tempting class hour. After all, we will begin the year as lab partners, and who knows what may or may not happen after such intimacy.

US history is team taught with English, and Mr. Henshaw and Ms. Brown teach it together. Gathering by the looks they send to one another, it doesn't look as though Mr. Henshaw is too happily married. I imagine this class will lend itself to a lot of great gossip, making each day much more interesting. I like to read, which should help, as the class looks as though there will be a lot of required reading and quite a bit of paperwork too. I hate to be bothered with all of those writing details, but I will manage somehow. I would much rather read and then discuss things rather than read and write them down. I know that is one way some people find easier to study for a test, but I'm not one of those people. I guess writing would be expected with a class teamed with English.

Finally, there is geometry with Ms. Azela. You can tell she likes what she does, and she is also the cheerleading coach, so I think I might enjoy math for a change. She always seems to be smiling, and is patient enough that maybe I will really learn something this year. I have always felt so inadequate in math, even though I have no reason to feel the way I do. I have gotten decent grades in it, but I always feel so intimidated by others in math class, and I am afraid to ask questions. I would really hate it if people thought I was as dumb as some of my questions are. All of the other kids seem quite at home with her and don't seem to be afraid to call out questions or answers. Maybe someday I will feel more comfortable about this too.

All in all, the day went well; I signed up for cheerleading tryouts and drama club, and found out when the play and musical tryouts are scheduled. I guess I am ready now for the year to begin. I wonder what extracurricular things Bill signed up for; probably Elaine Willoughaby 101. I need to set my sights higher. By his reaction to me in Biology class, he is pleased to be my friend, but scared to death to look me in the eye. Either he is crazy about Elaine or scared of himself and the fact he could easily fall for someone else. I know there will be some cool guys in the drama club. I will look forward to searching, studying, and researching that topic as soon as possible. Until then, I can focus on the up and coming cheerleading tryouts.

I wonder how the tryouts are going in Chicago. I haven't heard from Jonathan or Betty, just a text here and there. I like my new school although I still feel kind of lonesome for them, and I just realized I haven't thought about them until just now.

I know I am smiling and acting nice all the time because I want people to like me. Sometimes I want to shout out terrible things at people, but I would not dare. I would like to feel comfortable to be just me, but not yet. I wish I had a boyfriend. It kills me to see couples in the hall together kissing and holding hands. It makes me feel left out. There are plenty of guys here; there ought to be one for me. The dates Shauna set me up on were awful. I guess I will just have to let nature take its course, so to speak. Meanwhile, she is between boyfriends again, and that makes it easier for me cause we can hang out since I don't' have one either. I want to be in love again, but not remembering Jonathan daily makes me think I never really was in love with him.

Chapter Six

Rah, Rah, Rah

THE TRYOUTS ARE STARTING, AND I AM NERVOUS. WHAT IF I am not as good as I was last year? What if I have the wrong look, wrong voice, or maybe I am too ugly? I feel so insecure about myself, and I hate it. I am not used to feeling like this, and I don't want anyone to know. Shauna says I am a shoe-in, whatever that means, but she has to tryout again too. Maybe I will have a better chance if I try out for both the JV and varsity squads. I do not know what to do, and I don't have anyone to talk to help me decide.

Tryouts here involve quite a bit of sitting and listening to begin with. I was not prepared to be so quiet as we listened to the rules and regulations of being a cheerleader, and had to get our physical cards to be signed by day three; no doctor's signature, no final tryouts. Until that third day of practice, we could practice for the squad, but that was it. We also had other papers we had to sign saying we would follow the athletic code of conduct, and we had to have two teachers sign to say that we were good citizens. I might have a hard time with that since I just came to this school.

I asked the coach about the teacher-signing requirement, and she said a copy of my last year's citizenship grades would suffice. Fortunately, I had received all ones last year, which was the best you could do. I figured that at least in this area, I would be considered qualified.

Next, we had to return with a copy of our end-of-the-year report card, showing that our grade point was above a 1.6. We needed another signature from our parents on a paper, saying that they knew about the rules and regulations and about our trying out and would stand behind the school in enforcing these rules.

By day three, I finally had a physical and got all my paperwork turned in. My mom had expected something like this, and had made a doctor's appointment for me way back in the summer. I could not believe that she did this without even asking me. Where did she ever come up with the name of a doctor? Just the same, it was a good idea on her part.

After three days of grueling practice and two days of freshman cuts, I was still in the running. I had made it as far as day three of the cuts, and I had consoled myself with the fact that I had done very well so far. As they say, so far, so good. Perhaps I will make it after all.

Nearly everyone that was still left was a cheerleader last year, either at the junior high level or here at the high school. Michelle and I were two exceptions to this rule as well as six other freshman girls that I did not know yet that were still in the running. Everyone left, and all seemed pretty good. I met Michelle in my French class, so it was nice to know someone besides Shauna who would be at tryouts. Of course, we all knew that Shauna would make it because she was outstanding, but both Michelle and I were sweating bullets, wondering what would happen. We wanted to make it so badly that we were even afraid to talk about it just in case the wrong person was listening and it would give us bad luck.

Today, final cuts will be made. I hope that I will be able to make it through the rest of the day without passing out or anything. I could hardly eat a thing at lunch. My stomach is churning and rolling, and I feel as if I am going to be sick. I am so glad that there are only ten more minutes until school gets out and we can dress for the last practice. FINALLY, the bell rang, and I ran to my locker, threw my stuff in, and ran to the gym locker room, dressed, and then walked in a calm fashion to the waiting area of the gym. There seated before me was a group of very quiet nervous pale-faced girls, each of whom was sitting very still. When Ms. Azela entered the gym, you could have heard a pin drop from any of the farthest corners of the school because it was so silent in there I would have sworn that no one was even bothering to breathe lest it would make a sound.

Ms. A began by reading all of the cheerleaders who made the junior varsity squad and dismissing a variety of others. Soon, there were only eleven of us left to tell either the good or the bad news to.

"Girls, sit down," she began. "Since yesterday, when I was unable to decide who of the remaining eleven girls would be cut, and I should cut at least one, I have come to a decision. The school has agreed to pay for additional uniforms, so I want to welcome all eleven of you to this year's East Grand Rapids High School's Varsity Cheerleading Squad. Practices will be everyday for the first three weeks, and twice a week after the games begin. Congratulations!"

I was so excited I could hardly listen to all of the other directions: how to wear your hair and makeup, and keeping up your grades, setting good examples, not staying out too late the night before a game, etc. We also are required to ride together to the away games, and cannot mingle with the team before or immediately after the game. She is one tough coach. Shauna says she is more talk than action, and I should not worry too much about these rules. She is a stickler for the mingling stuff, though. If your boyfriend is on the team, stay away from him until we are back at the school, or at home, or until all the games are over. Wow, maybe I will be able to get another boyfriend who is on the team. Jonathan will be hard to replace, though he was so cute, a great kisser, and it was fun cheering, especially for him. He had not started to push me either into doing things I was not ready for, and I liked the no-pressure relationship. This school seems pretty advanced in that area. Shauna was talking about Mona somebody who had a baby in July and was back in classes. Everyone thinks she adopted the kid out. No one has said who the father was either. Talk has it that the father went to Wyoming High on the other side of town. What a creep of a guy to desert her in her time of need. It seems like he should have had to help her out somehow.

With health as a required subject, how can all these kids have kids? You would think they would at least pay attention to that part of the class. Betty at my old house had gotten her doctor to give her birth control pills when she turned fourteen and not even tell her parents. She, of course, had not actually put them to the test yet, but she liked to plan ahead just in case. Knowing Betty, she will wait until she falls in love first. All these guys she is dating now have not been THE ONE. I wonder how she is doing anyway. I sure do miss her. Mom never would have let me hang out with her if she had known about those pills. It is a good thing that we code messages on our phones so the Rents don't know what they mean.

Shauna's crowd seems even more advanced than Betty was. It feels good to be included with her group; I feel pretty popular now. I do enjoy her friends, and some of them are now my friends. All I can think about is that I have just got to get involved in the theater. This is driving me crazy not to be practicing for something besides cheering.

Shauna does know some dreamy guys. I will probably get to date some of her rejects. I sure hope that they have different expectations than the last guy she set me up with did. I may get myself a reputation as an Ice Maiden or something, but at this point, I don't really care.

Cheerleading practices are going great. We get to practice out on the football field while the players are practicing. We can all keep our eyes on each other this way. Jeremy Alva, tight end (what a name for a football position), looks pretty good to me…I wonder if we have anything in common. Shauna says he's in between girls, so perhaps I will have an opportunity to date him. She says she will introduce me as soon as she gets a chance.

Jeremy is not in any of my classes, and Shauna says that is because he is a junior. I guess he plays baseball in the spring; other than that and football, according to Shauna, and his only other interests are girls, girls, and girls.

The other girls on the squad are a mixture of sophomores, juniors, and seniors. This school has a JV squad for the JV team, and most of the cheerleaders for that team are freshmen. There are a couple of sophomores on that squad too. Cheerleaders have to try out again when basketball starts. In my old school, you were a cheerleader all year; a lot of unnecessary trauma to me. The coach says she doesn't make the rules, she just enforces them. We are told to follow them.

The other girls on the varsity squad besides Shauna and Michelle are a junior, Melanie, who moved here from California last year, and is still complaining about how cold it is here. She is extremely pretty and very shy. Meghan and Molly are twins, both seniors, and are co-captains of the squad. They have red hair and freckles and the cutest noses you ever saw. They have always been cheerleaders, and are really perfectionists with the cheers. We have to be perfect or else we have to do everything over. Then there's Colleen, Amanda, Cindy, Teri, and Olivia. They also are seniors. They are each gorgeous in their own ways; except for Teri, who is very stuck up, they are all nice. I wouldn't dare tell any of them a secret though. I might as well put it on the loud speaker. But I am enjoying my friendships with them just the same. They are all just like Shauna and seem to know all things information around school.

Shauna says we will now be invited to upper classmen parties. She should know as she already got to go last year. The only thing she warned me to watch out for was Teri and Olivia because they are boyfriend stealers. Their reputations say that they will do anything for any guy and whatever it takes to keep him, if you get the picture. This really surprised me because they did not seem like that to me. But as Shauna says, how can you tell anyway? Guys lie so much about these things. Right now, they both have steadies and do not seem to be looking for a new guy. I also heard that they give great parties. I can hardly wait to get invited to one. Perhaps I should be careful around them, not be a best friend or anything, but give them the benefit of the doubt on the reputation thing since I don't know if it is even true. I hope it's not.

I am doing all right in my classes so far, except French because I hate it. Somebody should buy the teacher a lint brush. She picks that lint off constantly and it drives me so crazy I cannot concentrate on what she is saying. Besides that, I found out that Bill is in that class, and I am distracted, sneaking glances at him. Once, he caught me looking, and I blushed. Perhaps Elaine should prepare herself for a letdown. Shauna says we have a lot in common too. He is in the plays and musicals. Maybe I will get lucky and land a part opposite him this year. Wouldn't that be something? I bet he would blush then! If it was not for Michelle being in my French class, I swear, I would flunk out of it. At least we can study together at practices just by speaking French. The other girls think we are hysterical. IF only they knew all the things we were saying! Perhaps we should be more careful.

Tomorrow is our first big football game against the school's city rival, Grant High. I can hardly wait because there is a dance after the game and a group of us are going to go to that together, then over to the twins for a party after. I am staying all night at Shauna's, so I will not have a curfew. I can hardly wait to see what the evening will bring. It should be great if it comes even close to my expectations! I know that some of those expectations might not fit into God's plan, and I need a lot of practice and prayer to patiently rely on Him instead of myself.

Chapter Seven

What Party?

THE GAME WAS EVERYTHING I HAD HOPED IT WOULD BE. The cheers came out perfectly, and I felt very proud to be part of such a great squad. It seemed as if all of our long practice sessions had been worth it as this was certainly a rewarding time. Our timing was great, and the crowd really got into the cheers and doing them with us. It was so much fun.

Jeremy looked up at me on one play and lost his footing. Fortunately, it did not mess up the game, but it sure made me feel good. Shauna introduced us yesterday, and we promised to dance one dance together. I can hardly wait.

To make the evening complete, we won the game on a conversion that worked perfectly. Even the coach could not believe that it worked. Poor old Grant High, they had not lost to East GR in eight years, and their coach was having a hard time congratulating our coach. Our coach, of course, was beside himself with delight, and the team was ecstatic. A lot of back-slapping must have gone on in the locker room on this one, and the crowd and the cheerleaders went wild afterward.

Everyone was really high on excitement at the dance. Shauna, once again, was between boyfriends, so it was great that we could go to the game and then to the dance together. Her having her own car makes it much more convenient. It was so much fun flirting with every guy there. I have picked up some tips from Shauna as she really knows how to get a guy's attention. She is even better at it than Betty was. I finally got to slow dance with Jeremy, who had a case of wandering hands. It was fun anyway, but he was getting on my nerves.

Earlier, I had a chance to flirt a little bit with Bill when Elaine was off at the bathroom. He turned red again, but this time he did talk to me. We were discussing the choir trip in the spring when Elaine showed up, slipped her arm through his, and dragged him away. He sure is cute...she looked furious with me as she glanced over her shoulder, glaring. I wonder if he'll be at the party. By her backward glance, she did not consider my flirting as inconspicuous as I thought it was, and she didn't appreciate it either. I guess I had better stop it for awhile. I know that I would not like it if it she were doing that with my boyfriend if I had one. Besides, I don't want to gain the same kind of reputation that Olivia and Teri have. Flirting is so much fun, but it does have its drawbacks.

Meghan and Molly said to start showing up around ten to their house for the after-dance party. Since we have to clear out at twelve, they wanted to start the party at least by then. Their parents let them have it in their basement recreation room, and we all had to promise to help them clean it up afterward. I can see why their folks were so particular because it is really nice down there. They have couches, a TV, ping pong, and lots of room to dance. Those two have quite a music selection, mostly slow dances, so Shauna and I got to dance some more. This time, when I danced with Jeremy, I smacked him since he asked for it when were dancing, and he straightened up. I told him I was not that kind of girl. He turned out to be a pretty good kisser too, and asked me for a date tomorrow night to a movie. I told him I probably would, but I would have to clear it with the Rents. Secretly, I had hoped Shauna would double date with us because I didn't want to be alone with him.

I do need to start getting back into circulation since Betty had recently texted me and told me Jonathan had a new girlfriend. I could hardly believe who it was either. It was Sarah Smith, simple Sarah. I can hardly say her name without gagging. She was so boring no one noticed her, and she was just so quiet. Jonathan's a great guy, so I guess there must be something special about her or he would not have noticed her. She must be nothing like me from what Betty wrote. Betty said she misses me. We hope to get together during Christmas break and swap information on our lives. Every once in awhile, I can sneak time away to text her or call her, but my minutes are limited, and I don't want anyone in the family to read our notes. I guess we will have to do more letters to avoid the families reading anything. I hope she can come to visit at Christmas because I really do not want to visit there.

The strangest thing happened at the party. It seems that one of the guys slipped something into the two-liter bottles of pop because some of the girls were getting a little giddy, and I got so dizzy I had to go and lie down. I even fell asleep for awhile.

Apparently, Bill took Elaine home and came back because when I woke up, he was next to me, and I do not remember a thing. Shauna said he did not do anything and that I didn't either, but I sure do not remember much. I am glad Jeremy had left by then. I do not trust him. Anyway, Bill and I had a long talk, and he held my hand and told me that he and Elaine had decided to date other people since they both realized that they had been tied down too long to one person, and being young and all that, they felt they needed to sample more of life. To make a long story short, I guess he wanted me to be his first sample as he was going to call me tomorrow to set up a date for a party after the next game, or just pizza then. He put his arm around me and gave me a great big hug and then he left. I should consider myself lucky that Bill was the kind of guy he was, who knows what could have happened to me after all the pop I had.

Shauna and I helped pick up the house; we were both feeling better by then, and Meghan and Molly were still sputtering about the soda pop mess. We never could figure out who put the stuff in the bottles. Meghan thought it must be vodka because that is clear, but Shauna thought it was whiskey, and Molly thought it was some kind of drug. I, on the other hand, had absolutely no idea as I didn't remember tasting anything different, and I hadn't even tasted any kind of booze or tried any drugs. All I knew was that I liked feeling giddy, but I didn't like missing that block of time that I could not recall.

Shauna and the girls assured me that all I did was sleep, and that they had thrown Jeremy out because he would not leave me alone. That bothered me, but they said they watched him, and he really did not get away with much because they threw him out right away. I was still concerned, though, because if they were giddy too, how could they remember everything and I could not?

After picking up, Shauna and I went home to her house and we were only five minutes late. Her folks were not mad because we told them that we had stayed to help clean up, and since we did not have dates, they didn't need to feel suspicious. They also knew Meghan and Molly's folks really well and could always call to check out our story, so they knew we would have to tell the truth. We did, of course, leave the part out about the drink switch. We would all be in hot water over that one.

I woke up three times with nightmares over the drink switch and thought about it all the next day. I think it was Jeremy who made the switch, and most of the girls think it was Sean because he seemed really out of it, like he had been drinking beforehand. I cannot believe the things some kids do. My Rents would kill me if they ever got wind of this, and I wonder what Jeremy will expect on our date after me being unable to remember what went on. I think I would know if something really big happened, wouldn't I?

The next worry was our coaches. If they found out, all of us would be in trouble for breaking training, breaking the rules of the code of ethics, and conduct. Sean is a great center, and the team would be hurt if we lost him. Being at a party where there was liquor is cause for all of us to be suspended, even if we didn't know about it ahead of time. We all agreed to keep our mouths shut and write this one off. Hopefully, we will pay better attention next time so it won't ever happen again. No more two liters, just individual pop cans, and maybe BYO pop so we know our own is safe and liquor free. None of us knows what to do if someone brings booze, though, because none of us wants to look stupid or babyish or anything. But honestly, we could all have been in big trouble. We are lucky Meghan and Molly's folks didn't notice either.

Shauna was shocked that I got two dates out of one party. She came up with one, so we decided we would work it out so we could double tomorrow night as I really did not want to go alone with Jeremy. I like him, but I do not trust him. He is very cute, funny, and interesting, but moves too fast for me. Shauna thinks that I worry about nothing, but just the same, she agreed to double with us if we could work it out. Shauna's date is with Allen again. He is crazy about her, but she says he is too possessive, pushy, and wants to be more involved than she wants to be. She doesn't want commitment, and he does. Hence, they fight all of the time. She hates fighting, but still enjoys being with him. He is really cute, maybe if she ever gets tired of him, and he of her, I could go out with him. He is interesting too.

I really hated the way I felt after having someone slip me that drink. It bothers me that I cannot remember what happened exactly. I am glad Shauna knew I behaved. Hopefully, it will not be all over school on Monday. We have all agreed to deny it if word gets out.

Shauna and I stayed up half the night talking about dating and guys and what they expect from you. I do not really know if she wanted me to know that I should be a little more free than I am or what, but I am just not comfortable with being that sexually open and free. Besides, my dad would kill me. Shauna, on the other hand, gave me some great inside ideas of how to turn a guy on. I am not sure I will ever really want to use any of them, but it's kind of nice to know some of this stuff. I really need more advice in the turning them off category. Boys almost always seem to be on.

Her parents have never talked to her about sex either. But both of our moms gave us the "menstruation being a woman in a nutshell" talk. They just left the baby part out of it. After the "talk," both of our folks gave us a book to read and told us if we had any questions, just to ask. Yeah, right! I am sure if I asked something, they would assume I needed to know for personal guidance. Get it...not that I was just interested. Thank goodness for friends and health class. Otherwise, I would still be totally in the dark.

We laughed over our own first discoveries. Both of us had once thought that you could get pregnant from dancing close or dancing in a bathing suit with a boy. Boy, were we stupid. I am glad I figured that one out. I would have missed out on some great dances! Shauna told me about her old best friend who moved away that had an abortion. I could hardly believe it. I never knew anyone who had one of those. Shauna told me some of the gory details; what a horrible experience for that girl. I guess she was really messed up after she went through all that, and her folks decided, when her dad was offered a promotion in another city, to just take it and move away. Shauna's parents never knew about any of this, just that her friend moved. She said that they would have freaked if they knew. I know what she means. My Rents would have been the same way. If they ever knew that we played spin the bottle at Betty's thirteenth birthday party, they would die. That was the first time I ever got kissed. Betty's brother and his older friends showed up to help us enjoy the party. They were right; it was more fun after they arrived. Looking back, I realize that we were lucky her folks showed up when they did because I think her brother Martin had more in mind than kissing a bunch of thirteen-year-olds. We were sure naive. Both Shauna and I are glad that we have matured so much.

She never really said if she had done it all the way, but she admitted to some pretty heavy petting and some things that I had not even thought of doing. I guess I am kind of a baby in this way. I know cheerleaders have a reputation, and she warned me if I did not calm down with the flirting, the guys would really expect me to put out. I knew that she was right, but it was so much fun. I should have realized that I was playing with fire, and you know what they say about fire: if you are not careful, you will get burned. I vowed from this time on to tone it down. I enjoy flirting so much that it will be hard to stop, and maybe when I meet the right guy, I won't want to flirt anymore.

Shauna says when you meet the right guy, you have the pressure of actually wanting to have sex too, and that your body cries out for it, just like the guys say theirs does. I find this hard to comprehend. I have always planned to wait until

I got married. You know when you go to church, that kind of thing is really ingrained in you. I can still remember several of Pastor Harmon's sermons on the evils of the flesh from back when I was a kid. For years, I was afraid of my own skin. It took me awhile to realize that he was not actually talking about skin, just your sinful self. Why can't preachers speak plain English?

This new minister at the church where we go now is not so much fire and evilness, but he does get to the point. They never actually tell you why, but they do make it clear that sex before marriage is wrong. They have never really explained why all of those great men of the Bible times seem to have more than one wife and many children when sex without being married is wrong. I still do not completely understand why, except for diseases like AIDS and herpes and a surprise pregnancy, that sex does not sound all that great. Still, I cannot help feeling curious. Shauna says that the girl who had the abortion used to talk about how great sex was until she turned up pregnant.

Shauna says she agrees with me somewhat, but there are things you can do to counteract your frustrations, as she puts it. As I have never had any of those frustrations, I have not even had to deal with any of the things she was bringing up, but it was interesting just the same.

We both fell asleep about 3:00 a.m., we think, and when morning came, my mouth felt like cotton, and my head and stomach felt like I had a slight case of the flu. I could sure kill that person who stuck that liquor in the pop! Shauna felt the same way, but she was not as mad as I was. She says it is always this way; you just have to learn to control and deal with it. She sure knows about things that I have no concept of. I am really lucky to have a friend who is so knowledgeable.

Neither one of us wanted to eat breakfast, so around 11:00 a.m., she drove me home. My folks were doing volunteer work at the church garage sale, so I had the place to myself for awhile. Jeremy called, and we set up the time and conditions for our date. He did not seem to object that Shauna and Allen were coming along. I was glad about that.

The folks came home around 3:00 p.m., and we had a long discussion about the happenings at the church. Samantha had found a new game and Sarah a new doll at the sale, and the whole family seemed happy. I told them about my date, and they seemed happy that I was finally becoming social again. They did not object and were thrilled that it was a double date. I guess they were glad that I was done moping around and complaining.

Samantha and Sarah were too busy trying to guess what my date would look like and getting into my makeup and nail polish to notice anything else. Both of them had adjusted great to the move. Samantha made friends immediately with the kids from her middle school who lived two streets over, and Sarah had two little girls living across the street to play with, as well as Robbie next door. It looked like all was well that ends well, so to speak, and, finally, I was beginning to feel comfortable too. This comfortable thing must be part of the plan! Yay!

Chapter Eight

The Date

Jeremy picked me up at exactly the right time and was quite a gentleman to my dad and mom. My sister Samantha fell immediately in love with him. I could tell by the way she kept staring at him and smiling. After introducing him to everyone, we left to pick up Shauna and Allen.

Much to my surprise, Allen and Jeremy had planned to go to a drive-in movie, not a theater. Shauna seemed agreeable to it, but I was uncomfortable. I had thought that we were going to go to an indoor movie where I would feel as if I had more control over Jeremy than I felt a drive-in movie would give me. This was our first real date, and it seemed premature to go to the drive-in. Even though I was uncomfortable, I went along with it and pretended that it didn't bother me. They had chosen a horror movie that scared me to death, at least the parts that I remember. I spent so much of my time fighting Jeremy off that I hardly saw any of the film. I had always disliked horror movies, and no one had even bothered to ask what I would like to see. They all just assumed I would like what they did. The movie was as disgusting as the company. I could not wait for it to be over. Jeremy and Allen had brought a cooler with pop and had brought a bag of popcorn. At the intermission, we passed the pop and popcorn around. This gave me a little breather, and I ate and drank very slowly so that I could sit away from Jeremy. Suddenly, I started to feel giddy again and realized that the guys had put liquor in the pop. Sometimes I cannot believe how naive I can be. How do I get myself into these messes anyway? I quit drinking it right then, but my mind was fuzzy, and I felt like laughing constantly. I was getting furious with Jeremy, who seemed to have his hands everywhere but where they were supposed to be.

I told Shauna about the pop and what I suspected when we went to the "little girls room," as she called it. She did not seem to mind that the pop had liquor in it and even seemed to be enjoying it. She must have because she kept drinking the stuff even after I told her what I suspected. She told me not to be such a prude and enjoy myself, and she even acted a little annoyed with me. I could not believe what she was saying. Boy, was I stupid. I felt set-up and humiliated. When we went back to the car, Jeremy was getting quite drunk and would not leave me alone. Feeling lightheaded, I was having a hard time controlling him and it was making me frustrated, to say the least. I was grateful that I wore my jeans with the buttons and zippers all over them, and since I am always so cold, I had worn a heavy jacket that buttoned and zipped. I could hardly wait to get home. Jeremy was getting drunker and drunker, and friendlier and friendlier, and I was feeling soberer and soberer, and uglier and more disgusted with the whole situation.

Finally, the movie was over and we started to drive home. I had not heard much from Shauna in awhile; glancing in the backseat, I could understand why. She and Allen were underneath a blanket, and several pieces of clothing were on top of the blanket; so much for our discussion of last night. Their actions spoke louder than any of the words that we had used the evening before. They did not even seem to notice that they were not alone. Jeremy acted as if this was a common everyday experience, but I was totally disgusted, and I felt used. I straightened up my clothes and hair the best I could, and when we got to my house, I jumped out of the car, said goodbye to the backseat, and thanked Jeremy for the interesting evening, and left quickly, running into the house before he could kiss me again. He did not ask to see me again, but I had not even given him the chance to ask, for at this point, I could move faster than he could, and I doubt if he would remember if he had asked me anyway.

I wonder what Jeremy will remember about tonight. And for that matter, I wonder what Allen and Shauna will remember. Jeremy had just better not spread any untrue rumors about me or his name will be mud. I suppose he will call and I will have a ready no for him. He is so self-centered I am sure he will not have the foggiest idea why any girl would turn down a chance to have a date with him. Looks and status are not everything. I could care less if I ever go out again with a football star. What a terrible evening. I was so glad that the Rents were in bed, and all I had to do was to tell them I was home. They did not get a good look at me, thank goodness. Looking in the mirror was a shock to me. My eyes were bloodshot, my hair was everywhere, and my bra was even unhooked. I could not recall how that could have happened.

I was really upset about what I had seen happen to Shauna. I could not believe that I could be so naive. The first real friend that I had since moving, and she had to be a mover. Did she really think that I would go along with all of this? I hardly knew Jeremy. What if my values were different than hers? No one even cared about my interests, values, or feelings. Maybe I will have to reevaluate my life, but not right now, as I have a terrible headache. I do not know if it is caused by the alcohol or the disappointment.

Tonight was terrible. I feel terrible about myself, my friends, and the guys in my life. I love being Shauna's friend for several reasons: one is that she introduces me to so many great guys and popular people. But what if they think I am like her? I wonder if she is easy. I guess that I do not know her very well after all. She was drinking and liking it. Maybe the other night was a put-on and she had something to do with the spiked pop. I wonder if I can trust her anymore. I wonder if she sleeps with everyone...I wonder what went on in that car after I left it. *Thank You, God, for watching over me. Something terrible could have happened to me tonight. I was scared. Jeremy was drunk, and he was driving. I was lucky to arrive home safely. He was drunk, and he tried to get me drunk and take advantage of me. Thank You, Lord, for saving me. Please help me, please. I don't know what to do.* All I could do was pray those words over and over again. I felt a sort of peace, knowing that the God who loves me would help me through this, but I felt friendless, but because of Him, I was not alone, though. I need to remember what is right ALL THE TIME.

I woke up in the middle of the night with nightmares about the evening, and suddenly realized that I need to get into a play. I need theater again in my life. When will the school musical be and what will it be? They cannot start tryouts soon enough for me. I will look into it on Monday; finally, something to look forward to.

The next morning after church, Shauna called to tell me how Jeremy went on and on about how much he liked me and how he could not wait to go out with me again, and how much fun he had. He thought I was so cute and cool and a great kisser. She never mentioned the incident in the backseat, and I didn't either. I asked her about the pop, and she said it was no big deal, that everyone does it, and if I chose not to, that was fine. She also said that I could not put others down for being part of the crowd. She actually saw nothing wrong with the entire evening, and told me that she and Allen were back together again and that he promised not to be so possessive anymore, and she believed him. He was so good-looking and so much fun, so how could she say no? He was such a great catch; he adored her, would do anything for her, and had begged her to go back with him. All I could think about was, *and is that all there is?* Maybe I will be counseling her if she goes and gets pregnant. She sure looked like she had or nearly had taken that step. She worries me; she is playing with fire.

The rest of Sunday was basically uneventful, and Monday was great. Jeremy followed me around all day, and I was civil but told him that I already had a date for Friday night and I was busy Saturday too, so maybe another time we would be able to go out. He seemed disappointed and tried to kiss me at my locker, carried my books, and tried to talk me into breaking one of my dates. He must have finally taken my word for it because he started following Teri around instead. The only difference here was that she looked as if she was enjoying it. All I could say was, "Good luck, Teri."

Back to Monday being great; the audition signs were posted. Finally, they announced in choir that this year's musical would be "Babes in Toyland," and tryouts would begin next Monday. All of the other information was there too, about practice days, songs, parts, and other necessary information people needed. I knew immediately that I wanted the part of Jane, and I started to practice the music and lines they handed out to people interested in trying out. I saw Shauna, and she said she was not interested in trying out, but Allen always did, and so did Bill and Jeremy, so she might work on the props or something so she could go to the cast party. She never ceases to amaze me. She can be so selfish, but I bet that we will have the best props ever made for this musical. She always carries through on what she commits to, but there always seems to be more to her volunteering than civic duty.

Finally, I really do have something to look forward to: a part and a date. I could hardly wait until next week.

Chapter Nine

Tryouts

TRYOUTS FOR THE SCHOOL MUSICAL WERE DIFFERENT HERE than back at my old school; you had certain songs to sing here and certain lines to learn. At my old school, you read from a script and could sing any song you chose. I had already picked up the lines and music that the choir teacher had handed out, and I guess I will be prepared with the suggested songs. "Toyland" seems to be the recommended one for this show, so I practiced it until I knew all the words and music inside out. I also practiced the lines. I practiced them with feeling, different voices, and finally, settled on a way of saying them that I felt comfortable with, and prepared myself for the magic day.

I could hardly wait to see who I would be trying out with. Apparently, they assigned you all numbers when you arrive, so you were always surprised when you began your tryout; that way, no one could practice together ahead of time and have an unfair advantage over anyone else for the parts. Most of the upper classmen got to go first. General knowledge along with gossip said that usually the upper classmen got the leads by virtue of their class standing and show experience, yet if an under-classman was better, it was up to the discretion of the director.

The choir teacher, Mr. Timpson, did it all: music, pro-ducing, and directing. Ms. Melogy, the drama teacher, was the drama director. Timpson handled everything with the vocal and instrumental music, and oversaw the direction of the lines, staging, and music. Melogy took care of the direc-tion of the lines and staging, backstage scenery, props, and makeup. They had a special choreographer coming in after rehearsals to begin to stage the dance numbers. The choreog-rapher would be the one to recommend the dancers for parts during the tryouts, but both directors had the final say. Our auditions were based on the choice of Timpson, Melogy, and this choreographer, Krystal Sheets, who taught dance in the area. The only one who knew me was Timpson, and so far, we had a good rapport. Hopefully that would help my standing rather than hurt it. I had heard from others that even if he hated you, if you were good, you could get a part, but he would be very hard on you if you were a thorn in his side.

After watching what seemed like hundreds of auditions of lines, songs, and dance that seemed all the same, I was getting bored. These auditions ranged from terrible to fairly good to two that were terrific. Finally, my number was called. I got paired up with a senior by the name of Tom Blue. Apparently, he had been in several previous shows and was not happy to be auditioning with a sophomore of unknown origin. He sang first, and I noted that he had a gorgeous tenor voice that nearly made your hair curl. Then it was my turn; once more for "Toyland." But before I could begin, the director stopped me.

"Serena," he asked. "Can you sing another selection?"

"What would you like to hear?" I bravely answered.

"Why don't you sing something acapella of your choice?" He said.

I thought for a moment and then sang "Where Is Love" from Oliver, a personal favorite of mine. Halfway through, Mr. T stopped me and asked Tom and I to go on to the reading. I was really worried at this point but did not show it and did what I thought was dynamite reading. I then joined the others waiting in the auditorium seats for further instructions.

The choreographer asked several of us if we knew how to dance. Most of us said we knew how to a little. She got up on stage and had me and several other kids, boys and girls, mimic her steps. Then all the directors said thanks and went on with auditions. Mr. T announced that the auditions would continue for two more days as there were so many kids who were interested in trying out, and the parts would be posted by Friday at the latest.

I was sure that I could not live until Friday. On Friday, as soon as the school opened, a whole group of us gathered around the board and saw that nothing except chorus and small parts were posted. My name was not listed underneath those. Beside the listed names was a note that said:

The Following People Should Report Directly To The Auditorium After Homeroom Attendance

There in the middle of the list was my name. I saw Tom's name on the list too, and that made me feel slightly better. Not knowing if this was good or bad, I read on and noticed that Bill and Elaine's names were on the list too. Maybe that was a good sign.

After I told my homeroom teacher I was there, I reported to the auditorium. There were nearly twenty kids all arriving at the same time I did. Mr. T sat us down and made this announcement.

"For the first time in East's history, we find that we have so many talented people that we are going to have to cast this year's musical with two casts."

Ms. Melogy went on from there. "Yes, we are delighted with this new discovery. Both casts will have two show nights. Cast A will have Wednesday and Friday, and cast One will have Thursday and Saturday. The Saturday matinee will be decided on later."

"You were assigned a cast by the way you interacted, danced, and sang. We feel that we have two very strong casts; one is equal to the other, and neither is better or stronger than the other one. There is to be NO RIVALRY between the two casts, or those causing the problems will be cut and replaced. If need be, each part can serve as understudy for the other part, though we are sure that will not be necessary. Each cast will meet at every practice for blocking and staging. In between, they will work with his or her individual cast on lines. Both Ms. Melogy and I will be working interchangeably with each cast, and you are answerable to both of us. Are there any questions?" said Mr. Timpson.

"Tom?" Mr. Timpson said.

"Yes, when will you tell us what parts we have?" asked Tom.

"Right now," answered Mr. T. He then read off cast A and then cast One. I was placed in cast One as Jane (can you believe it?).

We all stood around and congratulated one another, and Ms. Melogy went to hang up the parts sign in the hall. I could hardly wait until practice. In my cast, I knew Meghan, Bill, and Tom. I could not have been more pleased. Jeremy was in cast A, and I was glad not to be working too closely with him. It looked as if they had shuffled upper and lower classmen all over. Most of the major parts were taken by upperclassmen, but there were three sophomores with leads, and I was pleased to be one of them.

By the time lunch hour arrived, everyone knew I had captured a large part in the musical. Shauna was so excited for me. Her main reason for being happy for me was because of the great cast parties. I did not care at this point, as I was so thrilled to finally be able to do what I wanted to do: act and sing. The dance was going to take more work, but I was glad that I had once had dance classes, so I was not totally dance-illiterate.

I knew if my grades sagged, I would be in big trouble, so I vowed to myself to work on keeping those up. My grades range from 2.8-3.5 in any given term, depending on my interest, dedication, and of course, the class. I am always being told that I could do better by my parents and my teachers, but nobody puts too much pressure on me because I do alright. I have to have a life too, and I cannot stand studying all the time. What is school without the extracurricular drama, music, cheerleading, and BOYS? I could not live without any of them except perhaps the cheerleading. Time will tell on that too. At least my Rents are fairly okay in the grade department. I try to get a B- only once in a while with mostly Bs and a few As. That seems to keep them happy and less nervous. Besides, I want to be an actress, so what do I need geometry and US history for anyway?

I could hardly wait to get home and tell my folks about the part. They, of course, were happy for me, but not too excited about driving me to practices all the time, what with the younger kids and all. Fortunately, I worked it out that they would let me get rides from other people and maybe when I learned to drive I could repay some of those rides. That, of course, would not be until summer though, as that is when it's easiest to take the driving class, and I do not have money saved to take it privately. Oh well, that would cut into play practice, and I just do not have the time. So, now for the good news, Tom and Jeremy, Meghan and Bill, all get to drive to practice. This is going to be great!

Chapter Ten

Rehearsals
Begin

ALL WE DID THE FIRST REHEARSAL WAS SIT AROUND THE auditorium and read through all of the parts and write in staging directions. Tom did not seem so put out with me anymore, and it was kind of nice getting to know some of the upper-class guys. He offered me a ride home, which, of course, I took. First of all, we stopped at Sally's, a drive-through go-inside place, for a coke. I guess that is where all the kids go after practices. We just walked around from car to car and visited. Everyone was so excited about the musical and everything, so it was all smiles and happiness, and it was fun. Tom offered to take me the next night too and give me a ride home also. I was on cloud nine when I walked through the door. I sure hope that I am not falling in love again. I hate it and love it all at the same time. The Rents will have a fit if they think he's a lot older. I guess I will not mention it unless they outright ask. I can probably avoid most questions for quite awhile. I have had a lot of practice with avoidance answering, and if I attempt to keep them informed about what is happening, they do not ask very many questions.

Shauna called the minute I walked in the door. I swear that she had binoculars on our house all night. She had already heard about my ride home and wanted to fill me in on Tom and all about his life. Apparently, he is big in choir and usually gets the leads in every production. I had not paid any attention to him or noticed him in choir prior to this. He probably hung around the senior crowd, so I had not seen him. He was also on tour last summer with Workshop Theater, a group that is city-wide and has teenagers in it from all over Grand Rapids. She said that competition is tough, and you have to try out, get a recommendation from your drama teacher, and develop your own improvisation piece for part of the tryouts. She said that last summer, they toured the southeast portion of the US, and this summer, they will go across country all the way to California to perform in one of the shows at Disneyland for one solid month. Chaperones are usually college drama majors, and sometimes some of the local teachers go too.

Tom also has had five semi-serious relationships, all with girls who were upperclassmen from last year and the year before. He gets around, Shauna said, and also gets what he wants. She called him a man of "experience," and encouraged me to go for the gold, so to speak. He gets acceptable grades, and Mr. T loves him. Shauna thinks that Mr. T must like me too if he paired me up with his favorite male musician. Apparently, Ms. Kristal Sheets hit the sheets with Tom last year, or that is what rumor says. Shauna said she does not really know for sure if that is true, but it seems possible; just by looking at him, you could see why, he is so mature-looking and acts older.

All of this caught me off guard, but did not scare me enough to call off my ride with him. He is great-looking and has a voice like an angel. I do not have to believe any of that stuff anyway; it could all be lies, and probably was. Just the same, I had a terrible time sleeping. I kept dreaming about Tom chasing me around his car singing, "Where Is Love?" I wonder what that is supposed to mean.

My attitude about moving has certainly changed. I got the part in the musical that I really wanted. I can hardly believe it. I am so glad that we moved now. I never thought that I would feel this way. I guess either I am growing up or just learning to accept more things in life.

I think that I may be getting a crush on Tom. He is so cute, and his voice could melt even the strongest metal. But he has a questionable reputation, and I definitely do not want to be a notch on anyone's belt. I will have to pay better attention to this situation and see if I can separate the facts from the fiction part of this guy.

I am still thinking about my date with Bill. Duh, there never was one. He called to cancel, said he thought he was coming down with something. I know that his problem is that he has terminal Elaine-itis. I knew that those two would not be separated for long. I guess I should be thankful that she doesn't hold our almost date against me.

Well it is getting late, so I guess I will try to get some sleep. Isn't Shauna crazy? She is a fun friend though, but I do not know how much I can really trust her. I would really like to be able to have someone I can trust to talk to. She is great for surface talking. I have not allowed myself to get into a discussion that runs too deep with her yet. Well, back to attempting to sleep, as tomorrow morning is coming soon.

I can't sleep. I wish that I could oversleep, but I never do. I've had lots of bad dreams about school as it honestly has been hard. Things could not be worse. I am having some problems in my French class, partially because I hate it so much, and the other part is that this teacher is crazy. She lets us correct our papers in class. She thinks that just because she has one side of the room trade papers with the other side of the room that no one cheats. Half of the kids in the class fill in the answers for the other half. It's making me nuts. How can she expect us not to cheat when she leaves everything open all the time. I have even cheated a couple of times, and can hardly believe it. I have never cheated before in my life. It makes me feel terrible, yet everyone else is doing it too. I bet that she doesn't even look over the tests before she puts them in the grade book. She probably doesn't put the grades in half the time. She actually put Bud Becker up at her desk to take his tests. All he does is look at the other tests she has piled there, pages to a smart kid's paper, like Allison Whiter, and copies it. He is getting better grades than Rachael Shotz because he has a better opportunity to cheat. Poor Rachael is so upset; she studies, does all of her own homework, and she does not cheat. After all of that, Bud still beats her in grade points because he cheats with the hand of experience. No one wants to tell because we are all at fault, and none of us can admit we were part of the cheating. I wish they would get rid of her.

I don't know what to do. It doesn't seem to matter what I do, I cannot bring my grade up. I have never gotten a C in any class before, and I have always gotten As in French. This teacher is off her rocker. I can bring myself to cheat daily even if that's what it calls for. The entire class is cheating and not listening or learning. Why should they when she leaves the door open to cheat so easily?

The worse thing she does is forget what she tells each hour. Sometimes she gives our fifth hour second hour's assignment and is furious because we do not have it done. She will not listen to reason when we tell her that was not our homework. I have received bad grades because of her bad memory. At least right after that, if we have a test, I no longer feel guilty if I cheat. It sure seems as if she would be about ready to retire. She sure missed the boat on control. She doesn't even seem to really care. It is like she is living in another world. I don't know if she has Alzheimer's or something. I don't know what to do. *Lord, help me to be a better person. I hate how this makes me feel. Lord, how can this stuff be in the plan? Please help me to pray as I should, and be patient for the answers.*

Chapter Eleven

Academics?

I LOVE THIS PLACE. IT IS HARD TO BELIEVE IT, BUT WITH the exception of French, I am really enjoying school this year. They say that there is a first time for everything, and for the first time in my life, I can honestly say that I look forward to being here.

Surprisingly enough, not only to me, but to the Rents, my grades have been at the A range so far this year. This is, of course, with the exception of French class. It does not appear that I will be able to do anything to bring that grade up. She does not accept extra credit of any kind, and if you miss a test and do not make it up the day you come back, it becomes a double zero in the grade book. She sure is rigid about some things and very lax on others.

After the November conferences, my folks were furious. It seems as if Ms. Swaynie had only two grades in the grade book for her students. They asked her about that, and she gave some long, drawn-out explanation of how this occurred. They, of course, knew differently, as they have seen all the homework she gives, as well as seen me struggle to study on a daily basis. When they complained to the counselor, the counselor just shook her head and said, "We are aware of there being some problems, and they are being addressed. That is all I can tell you." This teacher is unbelievable.

My biology class, with the exception of choir, is the class that I have the most fun in. I love being Bill's lab partner, and we have become fairly good friends. Elaine has accepted this, and I guess she realizes that I have no personal interest in Bill anymore. When I stopped flirting with him, both he and she relaxed, and I feel better just being myself. Right now, we are dissecting frogs. This is very interesting, but smelly. I am glad that Bill is not squeamish because I hate the smell, but like the dissecting part.

In my English-social studies block class, we are doing reports across the curriculum. We are studying a country of our choice and bringing in ideas of environmental changes and work, as well as the historical parts of that country and how they relate to America. We are to include mention of famous writers, poets, and other artists from that region. Also, we need to include literature and other information about our country. Mine is on Spain, and right now, I am researching Picasso and the effect the Spanish Civil War and WWII had on his art; a complicated and influential painter. I love being able to access the computer for information, and I am learning a lot.

By the way, rumor has it that Mr. Henshaw is getting a divorce. I wonder if Ms. Brown has anything to do with that. We probably will know when the divorce is final and they can "come out of the closet."

Geometry is fun. Ms. Azela is very interesting, and she explains things so that even I can understand them. I am shocked that I have an A in there.

Last but not least is choir. Although Mr. T has a bad reputation for trying to date the high school students, I have not seen any of this activity go on. He can be a real grouch, and he yells a lot, but the songs he chooses and the direction he gives makes the choir sound fantastic. We are practicing now for the December program that we give. There is a portion of it in school for the students, and then at night, for the parents and the community. I am in an octet, and we sing, "What Child Is This?" The entire choir sings a lot of the old favorites, like "Up on the Housetop." This is performed with bells and a sleigh, pulled by four large senior boys dressed as reindeer. One of the tiny little girls in the choir is being dressed up like Santa, big and round. It is hysterically funny when we do it all together and great fun. It is a nice way to kick off the holiday season.

We end the program with "We Wish You a Merry Christmas." Balloons are supposed to fall all over us on the last refrain when the audience joins in singing. I hope the balloon stunt goes alright. We do not get to practice it because it isn't feasible.

So far this year, I am enjoying the fact that I am a sophomore. The year has just flown by!

Chapter Twelve

There's No Business Like Show Business

THIS PAST NOVEMBER AND NOW DECEMBER HAS BEEN rough for me in school. My French grades are terrible, and I can't seem to do anything to bring them up. Cheating is hard for me to do, even though the entire class cheats. This includes the kids who go to my church. I am having a hard time dealing with this, and it's making me depressed.

Fortunately, my other grades remain fine. I really like the English-social studies combined class. We do a lot of writing and taking notes, which is okay because it is interesting. They let us work in groups a lot, and I really enjoy that. So far, we have picked our groups, and I have been lucky enough to be with people who want to do well in class. We have had two major group presentations so far, and my groups have received As on both. My across-the-curriculum report is coming together just right. I am very proud of it and all that I have learned writing it.

The gossip is probably true about my block class teachers. Every once in a while, I think I see Mr. Henshaw and Ms. Brown looking at each other in a knowing way, but they are very cautious, as they should be. They are always together. If they are not having an affair, they are closer than they should be as friends, or at least that is the way it looks to me. So far, the rumors about Mr. Henshaw's divorce have remained rumors.

Rehearsals went great all through November, and I can hardly wait until December when we can practice exclusively in the auditorium during the Christmas break for hours and hours. The best part of this is that only cast members and the directors would be there.

Jeremy finally got the hint that I was not interested in him, and he began, if you can believe it, to flirt with Elaine. Bill let him know what he thought of that, and soon, Jeremy stopped and started on some of the underclass girls who did not know of his reputation yet. They were so impressed that someone older and so-called "popular" asked them out that they did not know what hit them until it was almost too late. The rumor mill was strong, but I knew for a fact that Jeremy was a lot of talk and hot air. The one freshman that I did believe had a thing with him was Marcy. She was a shy, cute and shapely naive girl. She followed him around and looked dreamily at him. He gave her just enough attention to keep her hanging on. She was so crazy about him that she missed all of the flirting he did with others. I caught him making out with one of the makeup girls one evening; fortunately, Marcy missed that night because she was sick. At one rehearsal, I did see Marcy and Jeremy in a doorway kissing, and leaving nothing to the observer's imagination. I can see where she got the idea that he liked her. His hands and lips were all over her. I sure would hate to see her get hurt, as she's so sweet. But maybe she is not as naive as I think she is.

Shauna finally forgave me for not being head over heels in love with Jeremy. She had illusions of grandeur that she, Allen, Jeremy and I would be able to ride off into the sunset together. After I explained why I did not like him, she still felt I had gone overboard with my prude act, but was not as mad at me anymore about it. She had Allen on her mind and only had time to think about my love life once in a while. This was fortunate for me. She and Allen were apart once again, fighting as usual.

I had dated several members of the cast; most of them were sophomores like me. For a while, I dated Mike, a junior. He played the part of Barnaby in the other cast. Mike was very funny in the part and funny when we went out too. We always had a great time, and we went out several times to movies, bowling, and indoor putt-putt golf. But as per usual, when I refused to put out, he became disinterested. At least I was not brokenhearted over the fact that we were no longer dating. I really had begun to like him just the same, and we had a lot of fun together. He was easy to talk to too. I knew he was not satisfied with the depth of our relationship because we had talked about it. After that talk, we decided that there was not that much magic between us, so he and I decided to go our separate ways dating, but remained good friends. I guess I was between boyfriends now too.

I had to try out for cheerleading for the basketball season, and had made the squad again. Everyone except Olivia made it this time. Rumor had it that she was pregnant, but who knows about rumors anyway? Her replacement was a girl named Becky, a senior and quite an athlete. I could hardly believe that she had not made the squad the first time. The other girls had said that she didn't even try out because she was competing in gymnastics with a club in town earlier. She is very flexible, so I can believe she is a gymnast.

Cheerleading was going great, and with no practices during the Christmas break, I could concentrate heavily on my role of Jane. I got into the habit of riding back and forth to practice with Tom and I did not even realize that we were becoming an item. We had not done anything except talk, ride together, and practice the script, and we had never dated. Rumors were really flying. We had not even held hands, for goodness sake. We both denied a romantic relationship, but no one believed us. I wondered if Tom had been making up stories about our relationship, but Mike said he had not heard anything, and I believed Mike.

There were a lot of other romances going on though. Elaine and Bill were involved again exclusively after they had broken up for awhile and dated others. I never did go out with Bill, though. We both knew all that flirting I did was stupid and didn't mean a thing, and while he was free, I was dating Mike. I figured he would be using me, and that it would be a rebound thing. All in all, I am glad that we never did get involved, as he could have hurt me, and Elaine would have been furious with me.

Tom played Tom in the play opposite of my Jane. We had our parts memorized perfectly as we had practiced the lines and blocking together. We had not had to do anything but embrace in a hug during our song, "Our Castle in Spain," and we had the dance memorized perfectly too. Then the director decided to change that and have us in a long embrace at the end of the song until the other characters, Grumio, Mary, and Alan arrived on the scene. Neither Tom nor I had a warning about this and perhaps because of the rumors, the director thought we would be comfortable. Tom was very self-assured, I could tell as the director told us to sing the last refrain and after our dance to kiss until the other characters broke in. I was so nervous, I could hardly dance, and I could feel my heart pounding as we tangoed to the music. Then it happened; Tom pulled me toward him and kissed me. I tried to remember to "act," and I responded back. We hardly heard the other characters enter, and the entire cast broke out laughing. We broke apart and continued to "act," though we did not look at each other. The rest of the rehearsal went on as usual, but I had a hard time focusing on what was happening.

On the way home, neither one of us spoke. I could tell he was looking at me, and I finally got my nerve up to look back.

"Want to go somewhere private and talk?" he asked.

"Sure," I replied.

His idea of private was a dead-end road that I had never seen before. I had no idea where it was or how we got there. As soon as we pulled in, he stopped the car, drew me close, and we kissed for about ten minutes. Finally, we stopped, he put his arm around me, and we began to talk.

"I have been wanting to do that for some time now," Tom stated.

"You have?" I said.

This opened the topic up, and we began to talk even more than we ever had before. We discussed the rumor mill, and he told me that he had wished it were true. I admitted that I had been afraid to even think about a relationship, as we had become such good friends. I did not want to ruin a perfectly good friendship by complicating it with romance.

Suddenly, I realized that it must be getting late. It was nearly ten o'clock. Fortunately, most practices had been getting us home around ten thirty. Tom figured that we had a few more minutes, and we sat in that car and kissed for most of them. I could feel myself falling into a tunnel that I was not sure I could find my way out of, and I was not sure that I wanted to try. He was very gentle, and we did not do anything that I had not done before. But why, then, did I feel so guilty? Finally, he drove me home, and we made plans to ride again together the next night. I ran inside, feeling very conspicuous, and yelled goodnight, and ran to my room. I had to pull myself together before anyone noticed my eyes and could read what was in them.

The first thing the next morning Shauna called, full of questions. She knew something was up when I would not talk on the phone. We made arrangements to get together in the afternoon. Right after she called, Tom called, and we talked for quite awhile. I had thought and dreamed about him all night, and he said he had done the same thing. I could hardly wait until 6:00 p.m. for play practice again. We decided to try and act normal so no one would suspect that our relationship had changed, but with Shauna already suspicious, I thought it was probably a lost cause. I could only hope to keep it from my Rents as long as possible. So far, they did not suspect a thing and seemed satisfied that I was dating around and that I had a ride to practice, and they didn't have to take me.

My shopping spree with Shauna turned out to be a gossip spree. She had a lot of things to tell me about Jeremy and Marcy. Apparently, there was a chance that Marcy might be pregnant. Everyone knew that Jeremy was a fast worker, but I had never envisioned this to be a possibility. I had hoped for Marcy's sake that the rumors were not true, and I hoped that he was good to her. According to Shauna, he was using her, but I had seen them together enough to know that he was as crazy about her as she was about him. I hope my folks don't get wind of this. I will be put under lock and key. They would go crazy if they knew about Tom.

Shauna said that the pregnancy rumor about Olivia was not true, but we both thought she asked for such a rumor, as she was always leaning on and touching boys and French-kissing practically every boy that walked by her locker. Everyone knew this as she did it right in the hall. She even had been seen in several groping sessions with different guys after school. I had seen her once by the gym before cheerleading practice with a football player all over her. He was practically undressing her right there, and she was not doing anything to stop him.

Shauna did not ask me much about Tom, as she had already heard about play practice. Along with this was the fact that we had not shown up at Sally's afterward, and after all, she knew when I got home. She just put two and two together and got her own version of four. So just for the record, I told her basically what had happened, and that I was beginning to really like him and that he was a good friend first. She probably did not believe me, but I felt better for saying it. She then reminded me about his reputation for the "Love her and leave her," a new one every play, etc., and I told her that it was not that way at all. Time would tell, though, wouldn't it?

After our discussion, I went home and got ready for play practice. After talking to Shauna, I could feel a damper had been put on my excitement of my new romance. I vowed not to let that same thing happen to me, and went cheerily to practice, glad that Tom was in my life.

As soon as we pulled away from the curb, he reached over and pulled me closer to him, and he put his arm around me. I put my head on his shoulder, and it felt natural to have it there.

Play practice went just fine, and when we did our scene with our song, "The Rain in Spain," with the dance and kiss, it went off as natural as possible. The director even commented on how much better it was than yesterday.

Tom wanted to go parking again after practice, but I put him off, so we went to Sally's and sat in a booth and talked. I came right out and told him what I had been told about his reputation, and he did not even respond to it. I was not quite sure how to react to his lack of response, so I dropped the subject. We then discussed a lot of other things. I still did not quite know where I stood with him. I didn't want to get married; I just wanted to be treated nicely. I also wanted to make it clear that I was not an object to be used.

We didn't say much in the car on the way home. Tom parked down and street and stopped.

"What are you doing?" I asked.

"I've been thinking about what you asked me before," he said. "I guess it is true that I have had a different girlfriend each play season. But it has not always been one-sided, and I have not always taken advantage of the girl I was dating. Some of them move pretty quickly themselves you know."

"Yes, I know. I was kind of shocked when I moved here, and I thought Chicago was ahead of the times." I said.

"There was a girl last fall," Tom went on, "that I could not get to stay away from me. Do you know that she snuck into my car one night after practice, and tried to, well, let's just say that she let me know she was available for anything and everything. I was uncomfortable around her, and it was hard to get rid of her. She was scary!"

"Thanks for telling me," I replied. "I don't want to be just another girl. Right now, you're one of my best friends, and I don't want to lose that."

"I know what you mean, Serena. None of my other relationships ever began like ours has," Tom answered.

We kissed for a long time, and then he drove me home in silence. Our feelings had grown so slowly over time that we had not been aware of what had been happening. We knew each other well enough by now that the silence spoke volumes without the necessity of language.

The next morning, Tom called me and asked if we could meet somewhere to go over some of the play. I asked my folks, and with their permission, he picked me up and we went over to the school. The directors were there and let us into a room to practice. Since we had practiced so much already, there wasn't really very much to cover. We had the script memorized perfectly, and the show would be in three weeks. All we had left were costume changes, whole cast rehearsals, and musical touchups. We just needed an excuse to see each other. I was happier than I could ever remember being. I hope I am following the plan and not making my own because I really like this part!

Chapter Thirteen

I've Got That
Holiday Feeling

THE HOLIDAYS WERE THE BEST THAT I COULD EVER
remember. I don't just mean the presents that we received,
but I enjoyed being with my family, the Christmas concert
at school, and even the extra church services that we started
attending because of that time of year. Both Samantha and
Sarah were in the church production. Samantha was an angel,
and Sarah, along with all the preschoolers, was a shepherd.
They were really cute, and it was a lot of fun to watch. This was
the first Christmas in a long time where I felt the true meaning
of the holidays in my heart. Love and goodwill to others was
flowing out of my ears. I actually felt thankful for that first gift
of the Christ Child so many years ago, and forgot to focus on
what I would be getting for gifts. My family was amazed.

My sisters received all kinds of things, but their favorite gift
was the two baby kittens that were under the tree on Christmas
morning. We had always wanted a cat, and Mom and Dad

finally let us get one. The girls did not know that I had helped pick the kittens out. Mom and I visited the humane society and chose two brothers to bring home. One was grey with long puffy hair and green eyes. His brother was grey with white paws and tummy and big green eyes. We had quite a time deciding on names. After a long session of agreeing and disagreeing and changing our minds, we settled on Willson and Kitters. I still, to this day, do not know how we ever came up with those two names.

My dad had surprised my mom with a weekend package for two to a motel in town, and they were going to spend New Year's Eve there alone. I somehow convinced them that I would be able to "sister sit," and they gave me permission to have three friends over for the evening to play cards and drink pop. Of course, I invited Tom, Shauna, and Allen. Mom had several of her friends on call should I need them, and, of course, they were just a couple of miles away.

After Samantha and Sarah went to bed, we sat around and watched a video that Allen had rented. Even though I protested loud and clear, Shauna and Allen insisted on being alone, and when Tom and I went up from the basement where we were watching the movie to get pop refills, Shauna locked us out. I told her if they were not back up in twenty minutes, I was breaking the door down and bringing them up myself.

Tom told me to stop worrying and then he proceeded to take my mind off the other two. Those twenty minutes ran into thirty minutes before I knew what had hit me. I was so crazy about Tom that I was having a hard time seeing straight.

All I can say is that it was a good thing that the house was full of people who could walk in on us at any minute.

After a while, I called down to Shauna and Allen and told them we were coming down in five minutes to watch the New Year ring in on the TV. When we got there, they both looked pretty happy, and I had to tell Shauna that she had her shirt on backward. Other than that, the evening went great.

At midnight, Tom kissed me and asked me to go with steady with him, and I happily said yes. Now it was official that we were a couple. I had not told my folks yet about our relationship, but maybe it was just as well. They would probably start asking a lot of questions that I really did not want to answer. So for the time being, I decided to keep my boyfriend to myself.

Life is perfect. Christmas was wonderful. I had so much fun helping pick out the two kittens for the family. Samantha and Sarah love them, and I do too. They are so playful and cuddly. They litter-trained easily too, and have not had even one accident. The Rents are still deciding if they will get them declawed. I guess it will depend on whether they choose to let them go outside or not. They are too little now and would freeze to death.

New Year's Eve couldn't have been more perfect. Spending the whole evening with Tom and becoming a couple was awesome. I am crazy about him. I have never been this wild about any guy before. It is scary and wonderful all at the same time.

Yesterday, Tom, Allen, Shauna, and I went sledding up by John Ball Park. It was so much fun. Afterward, we went back to Shauna's for hot chocolate and a movie. This time, when she and Allen split off by themselves, Tom and I didn't care.

We enjoyed the time alone just to be together and watch the film. It's silly, but we rented *Babes in Toyland,* and loved watching every minute of it. I think it will become "our movie." I am so happy I will split apart if I smile any wider.

It amazes me how much Shauna's parents trust her. They are never home and don't care if she brings friends in. I always have to have permission. New Year's Eve was the only exception my folks have ever made. They would probably kill me if they knew how many times we had been alone with guys at Shauna's. This is one case where what they don't know won't hurt me!

Soon, school started up again, and things went back to just the way they were before the break. Cheerleading began as if it had never stopped, and it took a lot of my free time. Rehearsals continued, thank goodness...at least I got to see Tom then. Tom and I had only choir together, being in different grades. I was starting to rely on him too much, and I could feel myself getting swept away. This feeling was beginning to scare me. I was glad I was so busy that we did not have much time alone. As much as we craved time alone, I knew instinctively that too much time alone wasn't a good idea. On weekends, we rarely went out because I had so much homework to catch up on, but on those rare occasions when we did, we always went parking, and I was beginning to worry about my ability to keep myself in control. Tom was great about not pushing me into anything I did not want to do. The trouble was not with him but with me. I did want to do some of these things, and I had to convince him I didn't want to, even when my eyes conveyed another message.

Thank goodness we still have play practice. I would die if I could not at least see him there.

I know I love Tom. Help! I feel lost in a spiraling tunnel. *Lord, give me strength.* Life is wonderful. He says he loves me, but can I believe him? I wonder how many times he has said that to other girls. I am too afraid to ask him. I have not told him how I feel, but he knows. I know he knows. His eyes convey strength and look right through me. He knows me too well, sometimes better than I know myself. I am happy, scared, and delirious. Life is wonderful, wonderful, wonderful. I am so in love I could die. Tom makes me feel different in a way that I have never felt before. I am having a hard time remembering to keep my values, looking to the vow I made to myself a long time ago, and to God. My heart says yes, but, fortunately, my mind says no. So far, I have convinced him that my mind says no, and I know deep down that it is wrong to get physically involved with someone before you are married, but it is hard to understand just the same. After all, we love each other. I do not want to be another girl of the current musical to him, yet I feel that he deeply cares for me. How can you tell if a guy loves you anyway? I mean really loves you enough to commit more to your relationship than to be a bed partner? Why is it wrong to make love to someone you love? Why do you have to be married first? If this is really love, why do I have so many questions?

Sometimes I hate it that my parents brought me up to have morals, to live by God's Word, and to always respect myself and my body. It would be so much easier to make choices if those ideals were not blocking my way. I do not know what to do, and I don't have anyone to talk to except to pray with half a heart as I fight with myself. I know God loves me despite my thoughts. Please give me answers, strength to stand by them, and allow His plan to happen instead of second-guessing everything all the time! As often as I toss and turn over these things, I really do know, deep within my soul, what I want, what I need, and what I should do. The problem is me. I want to ignore it all and give in. I am praying for strength to save me from myself.

Chapter Fourteen

It's Showtime

THE FIRST NIGHT OF THE PLAY WENT WELL. MY CAST WAS assigned Thursday and both Saturday performances. Our shows were fabulous, and everything seemed perfect. We got standing ovations each and every night. My parents were thrilled with my performance, and I finally introduced them to Tom. I still had not told them that we were going together. They looked a little shocked when I told them that he was taking me to the cast party as a date, not just as my ride this time.

My mom looked at me differently after I made the announcement about the date. I was unaware at this time that she and Dad had met Tom's folks, and apparently, we had been discussed. I guess that our respective parents had been fooled by our "friendship" and had not considered that we were more than friends. Then again, maybe my mom had her suspicions confirmed. One never knows about Rents, especially mothers.

They seem to have a sixth sense sometimes, and that can be unnerving.

The cast party was a blast. I got to stay out really late, and Tom and I danced and danced and danced. I felt like I was high on excitement and was not even the least bit tired.

Elaine and Bill were totally involved in each other by this point and arrived late and left early. I began to wonder about those two. I imagined that they would be engaged before we graduated. They seemed so serious already. Who could think of marriage at this time in his or her life? Not me, there were too many things that I wanted and needed to do before I let myself get that "tied down."

The continued rumors about Marcy and Jeremy turned out to be negative; she wasn't pregnant, but all signs of that being a possibility in the future were there. At least by this time, Jeremy really liked Marcy and wasn't just using her, so that subject rarely was discussed anymore. I could not believe all of the kids I knew who were sexually involved. But on the other hand, the majority of the girls I knew were not and had not been involved that way. It is a funny world when it comes to that subject. I knew for a fact that most of the talk was just that, talk. Oh sure, a few of the kids were involved, but most of them were like me. Sometimes I thought about it, but deep down, I knew that I was neither ready or wanted that kind of relationship, and anyone who has a brain in their heads knows that will never keep a guy. In this day and age, people do not have to get married, so if a girl were to get pregnant, she may be emotionally on her own; that's to say nothing about the financial burden, and thoughts of raising a child alone. That was definitely not for me.

Since my relationship had begun with Tom, Shauna and I had not double dated. She seemed to be happy about this, and even told me that she liked being alone with Allen. I was rather concerned about her. I wondered if she was drinking a lot now, or if that one time had been a fluke, and if their relationship had gone farther than Shauna was ready to admit. I would have to make a point to talk to her soon. She just was not herself lately, and with the play, I was really busy.

Tom and I were a topic for people to talk about. They were laying odds on if we would stay together after the play and for how long. Apparently, he usually lost interest in his girl-friends soon after the show was over. Shauna thought I would become another casualty and was always offering unsolicited advice about keeping a man; things like if I did not want him to dump me, I had better give in a little. Her other advice told me to drop him first. I refused both suggestions. She was convinced he would trip me up somehow and probably dump me after smearing my name at school. I couldn't imagine Tom doing such a thing, but in the dark corners of my mind, I knew that a part of me knew that could be possible. Either way, I was determined that it would be my way or the highway. *Thank You, God, for giving me strength.*

Tom and I left the party a little early, but not too early, and he drove the car to a private area where we could talk. Lately, he had been putting extra pressure on me and I got the "if you loved me you would…" and even though he had been very understanding to this point, it made me mad. I told him to take me home. We drove back in silence; neither one of us spoke a word or even looked at each other. When he pulled into the driveway, I turned, looked at him, opened the door, and slammed it hard and didn't look back. I was hurt, miserable, and very lonely. I thought at least he would call out after me, but he just screeched the tires out of the driveway and roared down the street. My parents didn't know that we were even going together yet, so I was glad I didn't have to explain anything. Fortunately, they were in bed already and did not hear the car, only me checking in to say I was home. It was all I could do to quickly say goodnight and disappear before they saw my face streaked with makeup from my tears.

Shauna called me first thing in the morning to rave about what a great party it was and how much fun she had with Allen. They were back together again after breaking up for the millionth time. She assumed that all was well with me, and I didn't tell her anything; after all, she didn't ask.

I made a mental note to talk to Shauna soon about her and Allen and why she had been acting so different lately.

Monday evolved as usual. No one had noticed anything different about me, so no one said anything, and Tom hadn't bothered to call me all weekend. I was disappointed that he was not waiting at my locker in the morning. I guess that he was glad that it was over so he could go on to other conquests. It was a good thing that I had enjoyed the play so much, or this could have ruined the experience for me.

It seemed strange that my best friend, later my late boyfriend, was no longer a part of my life. It must have been like giving up coffee or cigarettes or something because I felt as if

I was coming down off of something I was totally addicted to. Depression had set in, and I could not eat, concentrate, or sleep for any length of time. Then I began to crave sleep, and that was all I wanted to do.

It's over. I have come to the realization that it really is over. I know that what I did was right, but why does it feel so awful? When you do the right thing, aren't you supposed to feel good?

Tom has been the best most caring friend I ever had. I guess we should not have let love mix into our friendship. If only that stupid teacher had not made us kiss in the play, we might never have realized how much we were attracted to each other. Things would have been all right, and we would still be best friends.

I am glad that I stood up for myself. I think I was falling in love with him. Fortunately, he didn't know that. I know I am too young and inexperienced to make these choices, but I know that I really do love him.

Please, Lord, help me get through this. I know you have a plan, but I don't like this part. I feel empty. I have no one to talk to about this. I am tired of crying and hiding my feelings. I wish it was easier to love someone. Why do I have to be fifteen? I cannot wait to grow up and be able to actually fall in love, be in love, and make love without feeling guilty, ashamed, used, or unsure.

With a lot of prayer, I am starting to eat again. It had become hard to make up excuses to my mother about why I was not eating. Stomach upset, school work, I already ate, and I was running out of answers. I am glad my appetite returned if just for that simple reason.

Tom and I are still not speaking. If we see each other in the hall, we act polite, but I still can't look him straight in the eyes. I miss him more than I can say.

But, as they say, the show must go on. I will continue to hide my thoughts and feelings, never letting anyone know of the breakup. After all, there's no business like show business. I had proven once again, that I was a good actress.

Chapter Fifteen

Moving Forward

EVENTUALLY, EVERYONE HEARD ABOUT THE BREAKUP OF Tom and Serena. It sounds so much like a soap opera doesn't it? Neither one of us was talking, so people were quite baffled about the reason. I refused to tell Shauna too, as I know it would be like putting it over the school loudspeaker since she can't keep a secret. She was furious with me and embarrassed that, for once, she didn't know everything.

When I tried to talk to Shauna about her relationship with Allen, she got nasty and said that she did not have to talk to me since I refused to confide in her. I told her of my concern, and she laughed in my face. I guess that all I can do is to talk to her periodically about it and hope that everything is all right and that she hasn't taken that final step of no return. She does seem to look happier lately, and I have not seen her act drunk or intoxicated at all. I hope that what I am seeing is real and not put on for the benefit of others.

Lately, I've noticed that Allen has become more and more possessive with Shauna again. Once in the hall, I saw one of the student teachers from the math block come up and lean against her locker to talk to her. When Allen walked up behind them, I saw his face and it was red with rage. He grabbed Shauna and pulled her back, and started to speak before he realized that it was a teacher she was talking to. He did a good job of covering it up, but I could tell Shauna was embarrassed that both of us saw this. After this incident, she just tossed back her hair and laughed. I wonder what this means. What has gotten into Allen?

Cheerleading continues, and I enjoyed the practices and got my grades up too. Even French came up to a solid B. I was thinking ahead to spring break and what I would do. I had thought about having Betty come to visit, as we had not made a connection at Christmas, but she and I had already gone our separate ways, and letters and texts were fewer and farther between. I think that we both realized that we were destined to a simple long-distance relationship if we continued to have one at all. At least we were both able to accept this now, and had settled into life in our own new worlds. The choir trip would take up part of the vacation anyway, so I wouldn't have much time to get together. I suppose that was for the best anyway.

I still cannot believe just nine months later, after my life had been turned topsy-turvy because of the move that I have adjusted so well.

My family has adjusted too. My sister Samantha has made a lot of new friends in middle school, and she loves school now. This was great since she had always hated it before. She is playing an instrument in the band, has joined the jazz band,

and is first chair trombone. She has been on the B honor roll
all year, and my folks are just elated. Soon, she will be getting
braces on her teeth, and she is not even upset about it.

Sarah, being so little, has had no problem adjusting. After
all, she still has her blanket, her doll, and Mom, her three
favorite things. She is happy as long as they are within sight
or nearby some place.

Dad has been spending a lot of time at work, but he and
Mom seem closer than ever. I have never seen them so lov-
ey-dovey, and they are always holding hands and touching.
It is actually kind of nice. It is hard to imagine, even in your
wildest dreams, that your parents have sex. After all, they are
not so young anymore. But I suppose with three kids, it should
be obvious that something had to have happened at least three
times. What a marvel.

Mom has gotten quite involved in volunteering at church
and in Sarah's pre-school group. She has made several new
friends, and always seems to be going to a meeting somewhere.
Lately, she had been talking about getting a job. This threw
all of us a little, but she has found a secretarial position that
is just part-time, and has convinced all of us that it is exactly
what she needs. Of course, the money would come in handy,
and she would be around for all of us most of the time. We
agreed unanimously that she should go for it, and she told us
she thought we would agree, so she told them she could start
in two weeks. I hadn't seen her so excited in quite some time.
She had gone shopping and had purchased some new outfits.
I must admit, my mom looks great in everything. On top of
that, she has pretty good taste too.

I still miss Tom, and I think about him more often that I would like to. We had quite a friendship going, and I especially miss our talks. I had seen him around school with another girl, but he had not seen me. He did call once or twice, but it was so hard to talk that we hung up only after a few minutes. Maybe someday, we will be able to begin our friendship again. We had never discussed what had happened between us or why, for some reason neither one of us could discuss it or had even attempted to discuss it. I guess the wounds were still too fresh. I know they are for me.

Now I am dating T. J., a nice boy in my second-hour class. I had begun to get my life back on track. T.J. and I just seem to go to movies and Sally's, and don't have much to say to one another. He talks mostly about his job and his car that he is building at his grandfather's. It is nice to be going out again without being in love, and he doesn't seem to expect much from me, and I am glad not to have to add much to the relationship either. It is nice not to have to be without a date all of the time. It did not matter if he called or not, I didn't have to see him exclusively, and if one of us was busy, we did not go out; simple, a no strings attached relationship. He thought a lot about his cars, and I still continued to think a lot about Tom. At least I am not alone all the time anymore.

Shauna and Allen had broken up again. Shauna was distraught and would not discuss it. Her behavior was strange, withdrawn, and she had begun to scare me. I wondered what had actually happened this time, and I was bound and determined to find out.

Chapter Sixteen

That's What Friends are For

I FINALLY GOT SHAUNA TO TALK TO ME. I TOLD HER WHAT had happened between Tom and me after I swore her to secrecy. Of course, I did not go into detail. Suddenly, she broke down and began to cry buckets of tears. After she settled down, she told me why she and Allen had broken up. Now I don't know if I'm glad she told me or not.

Shauna told me that she knows she led Allen on a little because they had done some heavy petting, and he had touched her almost everywhere, but she swore she was a virgin and had never intended to be anything less. For some reason, he had other ideas and must have thought that she did too.

I guess one evening after they went out to a movie, he made his move. After they parked in their usual place, he went further than he had before. He had been giving her the same line, "If you loved me, you would" like Tom had given me, only Allen would not take no for an answer. No matter how many times she said no, he still pushed her. I guess what happened is that even when she said no both physically and verbally, he kept going on. He held her down against her will; while she cried out no, he raped her. Afterward, he acted as if she had been a willing participant. He had not reacted to her tears or her stiffness. She had been too scared to talk to anyone about it. She had not even been to a clinic or anything. She refused to talk to Allen, and she was scared that her parents and the rest of the world would find out, blame her, and punish her for it.

Sitting there with Shauna in my arms, we cried together. Her out of fear, despair, grief, and shame, and me out of care and concern for my friend, and hatred for Allen for what he had done to her.

After pleading with her for hours, it seemed, I finally convinced her to see someone. She would go only if I promised to go with her. So on Monday after school, we took the bus to a Planned Parenthood place that I looked up online. She had refused to see a school counselor, fearful that they might call her parents. She gave a fictitious name and saw a doctor on staff. I could tell that the doctor knew that the names we gave were false, but she was a good listener and told us what tests were needed and examined Shauna. Shauna was scared to be in there alone, so I even went in the examining room with her. When the doctor asked her specific questions about what kind of birth control she had used and if she needed a prescription for a diaphragm or birth control pills, Shauna burst into tears and would not quit crying. They tried to get her to give them more information, but all she would do was cry. Shauna was afraid to tell them what had happened, and I could tell by their questions and looks that they suspected that she had been unwilling in this sexual encounter. I told them as much as Shauna would let me, but I knew that was not enough.

The counselor tried to get me to convince her to go to the police and press charges, but Shauna just cried harder when we talked to her about it. I promised the counselor I would discuss it with Shauna again at a later date. Meanwhile, she had the necessary tests: AIDS and pregnancy tests and tests for venereal disease. We refused to give a phone number, and made an appointment to return in a week when most of the test results would be back.

This was the longest week of my life. Shauna and I had become closer friends, and she was leaning pretty heavily on me. She had started to drink some, and I felt that I needed to be with her as much as possible. This seemed to control her drinking most of the time because she would not drink around me.

Secretly, I got into her locker and threw out all of the liquor in there. To this day, she still doesn't know it was me who took it. She thinks someone stole it. She had black marks underneath each eye, and I swear she had not slept in days. She looked terrible, and she was getting very thin.

Allen came around, and Shauna cried when he left. The dumb idiot does not even realize what he did. I swear someday I am going to tell him off.

Finally, the reports on all of the blood work and other tests came back; no AIDS, no venereal diseases, and no pregnancy. Shauna seemed to relax a little when we heard this good news, but she was still not herself. I guess it is crazy of me to think that she could ever return to that innocent girl she once was. A lot had changed for her, and she really could not return to that lost place but must instead go forward.

I have been going with her to rape counseling once a week, and it seems to be helping. I know her drinking has subsided, and she seems more alert. We lie and say that we are going shopping on these dates, and so far, no one wonders why we never buy anything. I am spending a fortune on bus fares, though. It is a good thing that I get lunch money because it is all going into bus fare. This is a good cause just the same, and I do not regret one cent of what I have spent. Shauna really needed a friend, and I am glad that I could be there for her.

I have learned an awful lot through this horrible experience. This could happen to anyone, and the tragedy of it is that girls rarely report it. That means that sometimes the same guy could do this over and over again to other girls without getting into trouble. This part makes me sick.

I do not know what Shauna would have done had I not pulled this information out of her. At least one good thing has come out of it. We have become very good friends who can be trusted to keep confidences.

Allen continues to amaze me with his stupidity. He still does not understand why Shauna refuses to have anything to do with him. I have noticed lately that he has been acting strangely. Shauna refused to talk about this, but rumors say he is high on something. It is hard to believe that a star athlete would stoop to do something like this, but maybe he has. I never thought he would rape my good friend either, but he did, so much for my predictions. Perhaps I have been wrong about him, and he is high because he is dealing with a bad conscience. One of these days, I am going to talk to him, and, boy, will he be sorry. Better yet, Shauna will talk to him. Maybe we can talk to him together.

Counseling is helping, and Shauna is doing better. She is getting over the feelings that what happened was her fault. They have told me that I need to stop going with her, and she needs to take over her own life again. I was surprised that this was a relief to me. The first couple of days, I walked her to the bus stop and waited for her to get on. She is now going regularly by herself. I know because I checked. I had to be sure. Maybe someday she will be able to tell her folks about this. Lord knows mine are asking me a lot of strange questions. I know that my mom knows something is up. I just can't tell them. They will freak and probably lock me up or something. Besides that, I know they will tell Shauna's parents, and she needs to do that herself. The counselor said that is part of the healing process.

I am so glad that she told me what had happened. The way she was going, I think she would be dead by now of alcohol poisoning if she had not gone for help. I think she has this under control now and drinking does not seem to be a necessity anymore, but I don't know for sure.

It scares me that the counselor said so many girls go through this and do not have a friend or anyone who can talk them into getting help. She said many of these girls commit suicide or get pregnant or fall into terrible depressive and self-abusive habits. I am glad that this did not happen to Shauna.

My prayers have been answered. *Thank You, God, for being there for me…Thank You for helping me to be there for Shauna. Thank You for giving me the strength to trust in Your plan instead of my own.*

Chapter Seventeen

Choir Trip

THE TIME HAS FINALLY ARRIVED FOR THE SPRING CHOIR trip. I have been looking forward to it for a long time, but now I am a little apprehensive about going. I know Tom will be along, and I wonder if his new girlfriend is in the choir. I don't think I have seen her. I hope that he is happy. I am thankful that T.J. is no longer in my life, and I am a free agent again.

Maybe I could look at this trip as a new beginning. After all, summer is just around the corner, and I will be job hunting as I turn sixteen in June. I could use a little extra money for more school clothes, and I should be thinking about saving for college. I can really think on this trip, plan my summer, read, and relax, and no commitments to anyone. I should feel relaxed and at peace, so why do I feel so edgy? It is time to pack.

We are all standing around with one hundred students, chaperones, instruments, music, musicians, and luggage to board the busses. Indiana and Valparaiso, here we come. We are to sing at several high schools on the way, and end our trip in song in the chapel on Valpo's campus during the Sunday worship hour. We will stay all night in the church, sing, and return home that day. We are all excited, anticipating so many things.

As people got their things loaded on the bus and filed in, I found myself on an inside seat with Tom sitting next to me. There was no place else to move, so I stayed put. Maybe it was time for us to talk, after all, and I had missed him.

After the bus had gotten underway, the chaperone on our bus stood up and reread us the rules and consequences for breaking these rules. There were the usual stay together, no fraternizing, no drinking, etc. The fraternizing part sent a lot of smiles down the rows of students as if they would pay attention to that part anyway. "Where there's a will, there's a way" attitude was prevalent, and I expected to find some new couples spring up on this trip. I looked up and saw Tom staring at me.

"So how have you been?" he asked.

"Alright, and you?" I replied.

"Same," he said.

"Who's your new girlfriend?" I countered.

"What are you talking about?" he asked

"Blond, tall, thin." I answered.

"Oh, that's just Melinda. She and I are lab partners in chem. II," he replied.

"She looked as if you were going out," I stated.

"Nah, we did a couple of times at the beginning of the year, long before the musical, but the chemistry was never there except in class, of course," he joked.

"Oh." I didn't know what else to say.

Silence is not golden. Did you ever notice how silent silence is? It is a very lonely sound. For as noisy and crowded as the bus was, I could feel dead silence all around me. I was desperately trying to find something to say, but could not think of a single thing. Instead, I leaned down and took out my novel for English class to read.

"Oh, you're reading that one too?" Tom asked.

"You've read it?" I replied.

"Sure. So has every other junior and senior at the school. It's required reading for every sophomore," he answered.

This was great, something non-political, unreligious, and impersonal to talk about. We then got into a discussion of the characters and how they related, and what the true symbolism of the book was. Tom really helped me. He even told me the kinds of things the teacher expected you to know for the final test, like all the characters, setting, inner meaning, symbolism, all that stuff.

"Tom thanks for all the help," I said. "I've missed working with you."

"Yeah, we did have some great times, didn't we?" he said.

The entire rest of the trip we talked and it felt really good to have my good friend back. Tom didn't place any demands on me, and we talked a little about the break-up. Both of us realized that we were not ready for such a serious relationship, and vowed to stay friends. Tom, finally, with much difficulty and in his own way, squeezed my hand as he apologized for pressuring me like that. I knew he had felt bad, but it was good to hear him say it. We both knew that he was going away to college in the summer, and I would be here in high school for another two years. Realistically, relationships at our age do not withstand that kind of separation, age, and experience difference. We both agreed to agree on that point.

This trip was the highlight of my school year so far. I loved the play, but having my best friend back really made the vacation stand out. We sang magnificently everywhere we went, especially in the chapel. Hearing one hundred voices echo in a huge church really is overwhelming. I nearly cried. I was so moved by it. Many of us got to take communion there as they allowed most Christian faiths to participate. It was very special taking communion with my fellow students. I think it brought our group even closer together. I felt very fulfilled when I got home, as if I had grown wiser, older somehow. The best part, again, was that I got my best friend back.

Thank You so much, God, for helping Tom and I to get back to being good friends. I love him, and he is too dear to me to lose again. I will be satisfied with him as my best friend forever if that is what it is to be because just having him in my life is great, no matter what. Please give me continued strength to rely on You and Your plans for me.

Chapter Eighteen

School's Done-
Sophomore Year
is Over

IT IS HARD TO BELIEVE NINE MONTHS AGO, WE WERE JUST beginning high school as sophomores. Graduation is in two days, and I will officially be a junior.

This has been a growing year for me. I have grown in a lot of ways, most of them good, I hope. I have learned some things about me that I didn't really want to know. I guess I was a pretty selfish child when we moved here. I can see now that all I thought about was me and how this move was going to affect me. My folks were pretty good to me, considering how horrible I acted and talked to them. I know that side of me will resurface again and again, and I will try to do my best to keep it under control as a teenager; at times, that's supposed to be impossible, I think.

Learning about relationships is what I could call this year. I have learned what a best friend consists of. Betty was a best friend, but on a different level than Shauna is a best friend.

Betty was special but Shauna is silver. Tom, who is my very best friend, is golden and the most valuable kind of friend. I have noticed my parents, for the first time, in that they have a very special relationship. I wonder if they once were golden friends. When I look around me and see that a lot of my friends' folks are divorced: Jeremy's, Marcy's, Allen's, half the cheerleaders' parents, and even some of my friends at church, I realize that I am lucky. My folks do not fight or yell at each other. They seem to enjoy being together too. I hope that when I get married, I can have a relationship like that where we are friends too.

Even our family relationships are fairly stable. Sure, Sarah and Samantha get on my nerves A LOT, but we love each other, and if push came to shove, we would be there for one another. I would never miss one of Samantha's concerts, and she would not miss any show I was in. Sarah seems to look up to both of us, and I hope that we can try, even when she drives us crazy, to set a good example for her. I can count myself as blessed, and I should say a prayer of thanks everyday for my family.

This neighborhood that my folks chose for us to live in was a good choice. People tend to look out for one another, like when Mr. Patterson, two houses down, had gall bladder surgery; my mom took his wife to the hospital. Some of the other neighbors let his dog out, and still others took in meals after he got home. That is what makes a good neighborhood. I know that it is good, too, because we look out for one another. I sure could not get away with having wild parties or anything like that for someone would be sure to look out for my well being and tell on me. Other than that, it is a good place to live.

Marcy and Jeremy are still together, but I think someone must have talked to Marcy because she is being careful not to give the wrong impression about their relationship. She was very hurt about the pregnancy rumor. It seems as if Jeremy started that rumor himself just to make it look like he was a great catch. I doubt he will ever do that again because he had to apologize to a whole group of us in front of Marcy, as she threatened to tell something he did not want told if he did not tell the truth about their relationship. I would practically kill to find out what that was. I was happy for both of them though, that those were just rumors.

Allen finally saw a counselor, and he looks better. I still do not know if he ever told anyone what he did to Shauna, but I do know that he went into a drug rehabilitation program, and he is now getting help for substance abuse. He does not hang around with us anymore at all. I think that, in a lot of ways, he did pay for the terrible injustice he dealt Shauna. He sure got himself into a lot of trouble after he raped her, and his life has certainly not been the same since either. I hope it is because he knows what he did was wrong and that he will NEVER do it again.

Shauna is doing much better. She finally was able to tell her parents. The rape counselor met with Shauna, me, and her mom and dad. It was made clear to her parents that this was confidential, and only if and when Shauna was ready, should anyone else be told. They were also warned that for Shauna's protection, they were not to pressure her into talking to them until she was ready, or pressure me for any added information. This could set her counseling back, and Shauna was in a healing process and needed their support.

For the first time, I have seen her mom around more. She seems to be there after school and in the morning when Shauna leaves for school. Her dad has cut back on his traveling some too. Maybe they finally realized that work and social events are not as important as their only daughter. I am glad because Shauna could really use her parents right now. Her mom even privately thanked me for being there for Shauna, and she cried and everything. Her dad broke down in tears in the hall at the counseling center. I was shocked. I know that they love her and will try to be there for her. It was a terrible shock to them though, and they were quite taken back by such an announcement, as most parents would be.

Finally, at the very last minute, the end of the year, I was able to pull a B average in my French class. Michelle helped me out a lot with this, as we studied constantly every lunch hour. Ms. Swaynie made the announcement that she will retire in two years, which is two years too late for me, but at least I can look forward to my sisters not having her. Michelle convinced me to go to the famous "Leaning Tower of Pizza" party that Ms. Swaynie told us about at the beginning of the year. As far as I am concerned, that was the only interesting thing that happened all year in there. Despite the fact that she made us watch slides of her trip to France, the pizza was good, and we had fun. I was glad, for the most part, that I went.

My other grades were between As and Bs, and I felt content with that. My folks were all right about it too, only mentioning college in relationship to grades once or twice. I will probably take a class where they teach you how to take the college entry tests. Tom took one and said it was invaluable.

Tom is still my best friend. I love him, depend on him, and have fun with and talk with him. Right now, that is all I need or can ask for. I am happy.

Chapter Nineteen

Looking Ahead

AS THE FRIENDSHIP BETWEEN TOM AND I REKINDLED, HE began picking me up for school again. People talked a lot about us, but our romance never picked up, as we both were too afraid to lose our best friends again. We never ever attempted to kiss again, but we hugged whenever one of us was in the mood.

Shauna continued to pester me about Tom, and all I told her was that he was my best male friend. We could talk for hours about anything and everything. It took awhile but pretty soon even Shauna began to believe me.

Soon, Tom began to casually date Lorna, and I, Trevor. We doubled quite often. Neither Lorna nor Trevor understood the relationship between Tom and I, and they never quite trusted that we were just friends.

Tom and Lorna were dating exclusively, but from our talks, I knew that she was more serious than he was. She was unhappy with me, but that didn't stop Tom and I from being friends.

Trevor went on to play the field. Once when we were out and I was carrying on about my concern for Tom, he told me that someday Tom and I would end up married because we seemed so close. I just laughed at him. "You don't marry your best friend," I told him.

I dated a few other guys, but no one seriously. I went to the junior prom with Jason Coolidge, a friend of Tom's, and Tom took another girl, not Lorna, to his. We compared notes, and decided that we should have gone together; we would have had more fun.

Soon, Tom broke it off altogether with Lorna, as graduation was nearing, and she still had hung on even after he took another girl to the prom. By this time, my folks had gotten used to seeing a lot of Tom, and since I dated other guys, they never were bothered by our friendship. In fact, my little sisters loved him, for he always had something sweet to say to each of them, and he would play Frisbee with them and twirl them around while I was getting ready. My dad liked Tom too. He would talk sports and politics with him, and mom liked it that he was so polite. The folks never really understood our relationship, but they didn't bother me about it, and that was all I cared about.

Today is the day. My best friend is graduating from high school. My whole family gets to go and be a part of it. I feel privileged to be able to sing the Benediction with the choir in honor of these seniors. I have grown to love this school, the people, and my friends.

Tom leaves for college soon. I cannot think about that. I miss him already. I cannot get his leaving out of my mind. I have controlled myself. I have not cried. I know this is for the best. We are, after all, best friends. This will not be like it was with Betty. Tom has been closer to me than Betty and I ever were. I will not let this friendship slip again. *Lord, help me to be his best friend, the most perfect best friend that was ever possible to be. That way, he will be my best friend forever too. That is my wish and prayer, my prayer for today.*

It's time. My whole family is ready and on the way to honor Tom. His folks and my folks had become good friends too. They discovered that they were in the same pinochle club. I guess after comparing notes, they figured our relationship was just a friendship, and both families had become good friends. Tom had two older brothers that were married, and one had two kids. Tom, being the youngest, had everyone making over him something awful, and those two kids, nephew Chase and niece Tricia, adored him. I had a wonderful time teasing him about being the favorite child.

The graduation was beautiful, and as a member of the choir, we got to sing the National Anthem and the school song. Finally, we would sing the Benediction. The graduating seniors are historically invited to come up on stage to sing the Benediction one last time. It was moving, and I could feel tears flowing down my cheeks as I looked around and saw the same sight on the faces of many others. I had begun to realize how very much I had grown to love this city, the school, and especially the people. How could I have ever made such a big deal about how awful this move would be? It has changed my life, a change for the better.

After Tom's graduation open house, we had planned to go and visit other friends' open houses together. We had gotten permission to go, but first, for some reason, we went to be alone in the park.

We walked along, not talking, just enjoying the fact that we were together. Tom took my hands in his, and looked at me for a long time. I started to cry, and he just pulled me in closer as we stood there for the longest time, holding one another in a soft embrace.

We had become such close friends that there was no need to say much. We knew precisely what the other person was thinking. Without moving apart, Tom spoke in a soft, broken voice.

"You know I will text and call you," he said.

"You'd better! I'm really going to miss you," I replied.

My tears continued to flow uncontrollably down my cheeks all over his shirt. I knew he would leave in two days for summer school, as he had been accepted to Northern on the contingency that he begin in the summer term. I also knew that was nearly five hundred miles away, and I wouldn't see him for a long, long time. The reality of it had finally hit us both, and I felt an emptiness that I had never felt before, swelling inside of me, surrounding me, choking me.

"Serena, you know how much I care. I really do love you. Do not forget me," Tom said, clearing his throat.

"I love you too," I replied, tears running down my face like a torrential rainstorm in the tropics.

Gently, he kissed me, and harder still, he held me, and we both knew we'd never lose touch with one another, whether it be as friends, or someday, something more.

Only time and maturity would tell what life would have in store for us. The strength of the bond between us was too strong to be broken simply by distance. We walked back to the car, hand in hand, each reminiscing on the past, relishing the present, and looking ahead to a promising future, knowing God has a plan.

About the Author

MRS. J IS A MOTHER, GRANDMOTHER OF FIVE, AND A RETIRED elementary school and special education teacher. A resident of Michigan, she enjoys many hobbies, including writing, reading, and traveling. She has earned degrees from Western Michigan and Michigan State Universities, as well as credits toward additional teaching credentials from Grand Valley State University.

Writing has always been a passion of hers, and she has written poetry, pen pal letters to her grandkids, church Christmas programs, and rewritten many classroom curriculums to meet student's needs when she was teaching. Professionally, she has written plays, skits, and church curriculum.

This book was started long ago when she had three teens of her own. While most of this story is fictional, many of life's experiences, either from her life as a teen and later as a parent or from friends and acquaintances, helped the story to develop. Her hope would be that teens reading Serena's story would find answers to some of their own struggles; being faithful to themselves, averting peer pressure, and the value of showing support as a non-judgmental friend.

CPSIA information can be obtained
at www.ICGtesting.com
Printed in the USA
BVHW071622290421
606135BV00004B/607